Augustus Peel

Honesty is the Best Policy

Vol. II

Augustus Peel

Honesty is the Best Policy
Vol. II

ISBN/EAN: 9783337047603

Printed in Europe, USA, Canada, Australia, Japan

Cover: Foto ©Andreas Hilbeck / pixelio.de

More available books at **www.hansebooks.com**

HONESTY IS THE BEST POLICY.

A NOVEL.

IN TWO VOLUMES.

BY

MRS. AUGUSTUS PEEL.

VOL II.

LONDON;

T. C. NEWBY, PUBLISHER,

30, WELBECK STREET CAVENDISH SQUARE.

———

1860.

CHAPTER I.

CAN only two years have passed? or rather can those friends I left since that time have become so changed as they now appear in that short period? I had just arrived in one of those fashionable watering places so frequented in Germany, to stay with the Churchills. I found Ellen sitting near the open windows, listening to the bands of music that played beneath; she was gaily dressed, rather in the extreme of fashion; her hair no longer hung in long ringlets, but was taken off her face in full braids,

with the slightest attempt possible at a cap
composed of Honiton lace and pale blue
velvet ribbons. Her cheeks were bright and
fuller, and her eyes animated, and full of expression, as she came forward and welcomed
me.   I noticed another lady sitting with her
back to me : her dress was of the palest grey,
of some soft hanging material, merely confined at the waist by a silk cord of the same
pale hue, while her auburn hair was simply
drawn off her face hanging loosely in a light
brown net.   When she turned round, I
started.   Was it Valerie thus sitting in
that close companionship with Ellen
Churchill ? Could it be Valerie in that
quiet simple dress ? and Ellen so bright
and gaily attired that came forward to
greet me ?

   " Oh, Inez, what a time it is since we
have met !" said Ellen. " I was determined
you should no longer be buried alive ; but
come and join us here. You have no con-
ception what a charming place this is."

After Valerie had left the room, I said—

"How did you become acquainted with Valerie, Ellen?"

She coloured; I fancy she remembered how on one occasion she had said, that she hoped and prayed Valerie might never cross her path.

"We met towards the end of the season at a mutual friend's, and when, after this, Lady Falconhurst's cards, inviting us to a breakfast, came, I asked Edward if he intended to accept the invitation, for I was inclined to refuse it; but he wished to go, so that decided the matter. We often met during the last month we were in London; and really, Inez, I see nothing in Valerie to disapprove. Every one thinks her changed for the better; and, then, she is so [lovely!'

I admitted the latter, but listened without answering to the rest of Ellen's praises. Noting my silence, she replied—

"You shall judge, and tell if I am not right about her: remember, now she is

married, much that was objectionable and
disagreeable, may have worn off. She is
so calm and gentle, and *very* serious, I assure you, Inez. Sometimes I feel quite
wicked, in comparison with her; perhaps
her opinions on religion border too closely
on the Roman Catholic doctrines to please
me; but she is sincere in what she says."

When Ellen paused, I felt rather weary
of listening to details of Valerie's goodness,
and asked how Mr. Churchill was, and if he
was at home.

" He will be in very soon," she said, " he
has ridden with Lord Falconhurst, to explore some pine forest near here. I often
ride with them, and so does Valerie. We
are out almost every night, and know all
the best people."

" And you are both looking better and
more cheerful," I said.

" Yes, decidedly," answered Ellen. " I
knew Edward was not the sort of man to
mope about in a quiet village, and to tell

you the truth, I began to dislike it also. We both grew so dull, that we left home, and visited different friends, and have passed two gay delightful seasons in London, which I enjoyed extremely. You must tell me presently, when you are rested, all you have been doing during these two years. We are going to a ball this evening. You will accompany us, I hope."

" Yes, certainly," I answered. " How glad I am to see you so happy, Ellen!"

She slightly turned from me, and with a laugh, replied—

" Yes, I told you when Edward was happy, you would never see a shadow on my brow. Edward once, as you know, did not care for society ; but I assure you *now*, he is never happy but in one whirl of excitement. Your cousin Valerie is the *belle* here. You cannot think what a fuss her husband makes about her ; and as for all the gentlemen; it's something quite amusing, when she enters a room, to see the crowds that surround her."

" I can quite imagine it," I said quietly, as I followed Ellen to the drawing-room.

Edward Churchill was sitting by Valerie, who read aloud to him. He turned very suddenly round, and coming up to me, said—

" Well, Inez, I am very glad you have come at last; and to add to the charm of this pleasant spot, your cousin, Lady Falconhurst has graced it with her presence."

" How absurd you are, Mr. Churchill," said Valerie, the same loud laugh, harsh and unmusical, echoing through the room. Yet, she was more beautiful than formerly; and there was more repose in her manner, a grace she had wanted before.

" Do not, let me prevent the reading," I said.

Valerie hesitated, cast one glance at Mr. Churchill from her lovely eyes, as much as

to ask, shall I proceed? while his gaze
deepening into one of intense admiration,
answered, if you are not tired. She took
up a volume of that beautiful and interesting book " Grantly Manor," then, glancing
at me, said—

" But I forgot, Inez will not listen to it;
there are some allusions, I think, to pictures, Saints, and Roman Catholics, of
which I know she highly disapproves.

" Inez knows so much about it," answered
Mr. Churchill.   His tone was sarcastic, but,
in the place of sullen looks and gloom of
manner a light gay tone was visible in all he
he said and did. I merely answered that the
book was a favourite of mine, and very interesting. Would she read on? As she
read, his eyes, and Ellen's too, I fancied,
rested on her, till they thought her like that
sweet saint—like Genevra—in her light loose
dress, so simple, so pure-looking; the very
classical turn of her features; the ripples
of sunny hair waving from her brow; the

soft long eyelashes; the small red lips; yes,
Valerie, to outward seeming you were beautiful.   Oh! for the heart within! and the
reading continued.   Ellen cast a fond happy
glance on her husband, and taking a low
seat near the ground, listened attentively
till Lord Falconhurst entered the room, and
the book was cast aside.

Edward Churchill's manner was open and
pleasant.   I seemed to lose the painful reserve I had at first felt in seeing him, and
soon became happy and at my ease. The ball
was very gay and I enjoyed it extremely.
Valerie and Ellen reigned supreme: both
received much attention; one, from a love
of it that never could be satisfied—for her
own self love; the other, from the mere
feeling that it made her husband proud and
satisfied with her.   Ellen therefore danced
gaily and naturally: Valerie refused to .
dance: she sat on a sofa, looking beautiful
in a white crape dress and a single rose in
her hair, surrounded by a crowd of adorers;

but there was, as Ellen had said to me, no
lightness of manner or appearance of flirt-
ing ; nothing that the strictest could disapprove; but a quiet smile on one ; a word of
flattery falling softly on another's ear; a
glance of her approval on some favoured one,
kept them all within her circle that she cared
to fascinate.   Edward Churchill was the
favourite.   He sat near her almost the
whole night; gay and handsome he looked,
too ; yet, something there was in his manner
conveying the idea of unhappiness : there
was no rest for him ; no peace ; he was not
happy ; Ellen might think he was; half
the world might have singled him out as an
especially joyous person, but he did not
seem so to me.

Lord and Lady Falconhurst living next
door, it seemed like one family.   Ellen and
Valerie were always together.   I saw this
intimacy spring up with great anxiety, but
I could easily understand it.   Valerie, rich,
of high rank, beautiful, and highly gifted,

and liking Edward Churchill's apparent attention, knew well how to insinuate herself into Ellen's weak, yielding nature. Entering eagerly into all her pursuits; lavishing caresses on her, and flattering her greatly, I soon perceived that my affection was as nothing compared with Valerie's, nor could she conceal it from me. I could not speak of it to her. As each day glided swiftly by I felt the estrangement grow wider and wider, till it seemed as though a gulf rolled betwixt us that could never be removed. I think, because I could not speak of this, it rankled deeper in my heart.

One morning, as I was dressing for a picnic, Ellen came into my room. She was still kind and thoughtful for me, and had come to see if I needed anything; wearing a loose morning dress, and with her hair hanging round her face, she looked like the Ellen I had first known. I said it brought back old times, seeing her thus.

" Yes, but I could not wear it in ringlets

now; I am changed, and so is my hair,"
she answered, laughing.

" Yes," I answered, looking at her ;
there might have passed over my face a
shade of grief, for quickly she rejoined—

" Changed, but not to you, Inez, dear !"
and she put her arm fondly round my neck.
It was with great difficulty I could bear all
I felt without giving it utterance ; I could
have flung my gay dress aside and wept my
very life away in bitter tears.

" There's ample time yet," she said, " let
us have a talk *now*, for you have never told
me of your Scotch visit."

" I wrote several times," I replied, " but
you seldom answered my letters."

" Ah ! I was very naughty," she said,
interrupting me, " and I am ashamed of
being such a bad correspondent, but really
my time was so fully occupied, particularly in
London, that I could not manage to write."

" I have not much to tell you in the way
of incident. The Mackensies were all

kindness to me, and I passed a quiet happy time with them ; I made several friends while there, who invited me to stay at their different Highland homes ; so it was late in the following summer when I returned to England."

" You saw Charlie while there," said Ellen, " for in all his letters he mentioned you."

" Yes, I saw him continually, and liked him very much."

Ellen, after a pause of some minutes, said—

" He never told me anything, believe me, Inez, of what passed between you ; but mamma mentioned, in one of her letters, something that pained me very much. I fear," she added, hesitatingly, " that mamma has behaved as strangely and unkindly in this affair as she did in ours."

" Not kindly, dear Ellen, certainly," I answered ; " but we must hope that this fancy of your brother's will pass off; he is very young yet, and it is best as it is."

Ellen gave a long sigh, but did not speak; she merely kissed me; perhaps she thought a first attachment was not so easily overcome.

" Where is your brother?" I asked.

" Still roaming about the world, I do not know where at this present moment," answered Ellen; " but let us come down stairs when we are dressed, for I hear Valerie and Edward singing together; he likes her so much, and really you cannot imagine the good she does in amusing and cheering him, and not only *that*, but I think her influence over him is good. Are you not delighted to see the change in her?"

" I must wait till I have seen it, to answer your question, Ellen: my own opinion is, that she is just as fond of admiration as when we parted, and I fancy she does not care the least for her husband, nor he for

her, more than being very proud of a beautiful and clever wife."

"You are unjust to her," said Ellen,
colouring; "I could give you a thousand
proofs of her goodness, but I perceive it
would be useless to do so. She never
neglects her duty: after being up nearly all
night Valerie will rise at an early hour and
attend the morning service."

I remained silent, but *thought* of the
curates.

"If you do not believe it, ask Edward,"
continued Ellen, rather warmly, "for he
has met her going to church."

"Does Mr. Churchill attend the service
before breakfast?" I asked.

Whether a smile I could scarcely restrain
annoyed Ellen, I don't know: she merely
replied, no, but he had met her when he
chanced to be out early in the morning;
and looking displeased, she left the room.

CHAPTER II.

AND many weeks glided by: living in one vortex of gaiety, what time was there to think or reflect on what passed around us? Never alone, either morning or evening, where had I time to feel either gay or miserable? and bad as this life might be for both mind and body, I would have it thus, rather than have it become a mere quiet family party; where every look and word would have been noticed and talked over. I knew well that while Valerie gained all the admiration, and had Mr. Churchill's attention, she would scarcely trouble herself

to notice me ; this was very comforting ; and
the only thing that caused me any uneasiness,
was, the power that she had gained over
Ellen.   Whatever Valerie wished was done
immediately ; any people she liked were invited to Mrs. Churchill's.   She was, in
Ellen's eyes, the standard of manners, cleverness, and amiability even : what she admired
in dress was instantly adopted.   Valerie, too,
had managed to bring Ellen into great notice,
by making her of importance, and talking of
her as a reigning belle ; and, although Ellen
had no real vanity at heart, I think she felt
the difference of having been in a measure
unnoticed, and now being raised in others'
estimation, and in her husband's also, as she
thought.   Valerie had no fear of Ellen as a
rival : she knew how really weak and powerless she was; and with her usual quickness
soon discovered, that though Ellen's heart
was centred in her husband, he was perfectly
indifferent to her.

Edward seldom spoke to, or appeared to

notice me in any way. Sometimes a hasty
glance, a restless air, told me that the life he
led was artificial, and gave him no real joy;
but that he had determined to continue it, I
felt assured; his liking for Valerie, too, was
strange: that she pleased and amused him,
was certain; and that he admired her, was
very evident; but there was no real interest
in her: she possessed no power over him;
she was a beauty, and flattered him; he,
being a man, could not resist *that.*

"I cannot imagine, Inez," exclaimed
Valerie, one day, " why you should have so
disliked Mr. Churchill: I declare, that had
I been left a whole summer with him as you
were, I should have fallen deeply in love;
yet, Ellen tells me, with such a grave face,
that she grieved to say that you did not even
like her husband; and that you were afraid
of him: I told her not to be such a little
goose, as I could not believe a word of it;
but she firmly avowed it to be the case: can
it be true?"

" No," I replied, " Ellen has always fancied
I disliked Mr. Churchill, but it is not the
case, and I have repeatedly told her so."

As I answered this question, Valerie looked
across the table at me, and said—

" Ah, well, you did not hate him quite so
much as Ellen thinks after all."

She smiled to herself, but remained silent.
When Ellen entered the room with a drawing
in her hand which she had just finished.

" What a sweet sketch," said Valerie;
" but that reminds me, Nelly darling, to ask
you if you would like your picture taken. I
am longing to possess one of you: so say
yes; I know what your answer will be—if
Edward likes it: now, he would like it very
much, for I asked him the other day."

" But who is to do it?" asked Ellen.

Valerie turned her head slightly from me,
as she answered in a composed tone of
voice—

" Why, there is a young artist coming to
stay with us to-morrow, a very rising young

man. He did the picture of me that you saw in London, and admired so much."

" Oh ! then, decidedly, I should like mine taken," said Ellen, " for it is one of the most beautiful pictures I ever saw, and so like you! I hope I shall prevail on Edward to have his done also. What is this artist's name ?

" Mr. Daubeney," Valerie replied. He is very clever, and a gentleman ; his mother was an Italian lady, highly connected, and extremely beautiful I have heard ; his father an Englishman of good family, but poor."

I raised my eyes to Valerie's ; hers looked boldly, steadily into mine. Yet, that I knew something of the past, was plain to her ; and I think her dislike of me strengthened and deepened in consequence. I knew that she had cared for Mr. Daubeney ; the only real feeling I had ever seen her evince was for him ; and that she had other motives for asking him to Germany than to take like-nesses, I felt assured. What would this violent friendship of Ellen's lead to ? and

where would it end? If I had thought that
words or warning would have availed, she
should not have been left entirely under the
guidance of one so thoroughly unprincipled; but I knew how vain both would be
now; and I waited and watched with anxiety
the end of all I looked on with wonder.

When Edward Churchill joined us, Valerie
talked for some time about the pictures,
pitying poor Mr. Daubeney, hoping Mr.
Churchill would recommend him highly.
She always felt for people in that painful
position, and should be glad to help him;
he had told her of his having entirely to
support two little sisters; it was altogether
so praiseworthy of him, highly born as he
was, and with sensitive feelings, to be now a
dependent upon others, struggling for his
livelihood. All this was spoken with such a
sincere air of pity and of kindness, that
Mr. Churchill said, such words as she had
just uttered would do more for Mr. Daubeney's success, with most people, than all

the letters and recommendations in the world.   I had sat listening to all this, and looking at Ellen's face ; she was gazing on Valerie, as if she were some saint that had uttered these words of kindness ; while Mr. Churchill, I could see, knew enough of Valerie, to feel that a great deal of what she said and did was for effect, and that perhaps some little interest on her own part for Mr. Daubeney influenced her to speak thus warmly in his favour.   There was a smile on his face as he turned towards me, and said,

" Why should not you have your picture done, Inez?   I should like it taken just as you are, in that white dress."

There was such a strange deep sadness in his glance as he fixed his eyes on me, that I thought of the summer evening when he had said, " there you stand in your shadowy white dress, like some spirit leading me on ;' and when he had bidden me sit on the beach beside him.   All the past came back to me

at that moment.   I coloured and remained
silent.

" Yes, Inez, have it done," said Ellen.

Valerie turned towards Mr. Churchill and
then to me.

Oh! what a contemptuous expression
darkened her face, as she said—

" As Mr. Churchill is so anxious, Inez, to
have you taken in that tumbled white dress,
why don't you agree at once, and not sit
blushing there."

" There will be time enough for me to
have it done, when we see the other pictures
finished," I replied coldly.

Mr, Churchill seemed still thinking of
Valerie's last words, for he said—

" I don't know if Miss Wentworth's dress
is tumbled or not; I only think it particularly becoming; and, as I intend to have
her likeness taken at my own expense, I
shall have it done in that dress."

He left the room; and Valerie, with her

face calm, but her eyelids trembling with suppressed anger, said—

" Ellen, darling, I never knew Mr. Churchill was so touchy on the subject of white dresses ; we must be more particular another time. I suppose that Inez' dislike to Mr. Churchill was shown in her silence just now. You should endeavour to overcome this violent hatred to your guardian," she continued, looking at me.

" Pray, Valerie, do not speak on this subject," interrupted Ellen, suddenly ; " and, as she has endeavoured to overcome her dislike to Edward, don't let us lecture her any more."

Valerie began laughing vehemently ; so much so, that Ellen looked perfectly astonished and confused ; and, on asking what caused such extreme merriment, Valerie only answered affectedly—

" Never mind, dear, only I cannot help laughing ; people see things so differently, no matter."

She laid her work down, and, turning to the piano, commenced singing. Mr. Churchill usually joined her, and their voices, both rich and powerful, blended well together; but, on that occasion, he did not appear; and Valerie, finding it was not his intention to do so, left the room. When I spoke to Ellen, she seemed absent in mind, evidently thinking deeply. I wondered if Valerie's words or laughter had raised any suspicion of the truth; whether some gleam of light shone for the first time through the cloud in which she had so long been enveloped. Would that any but Valerie could have drawn the veil! her deadly influence would be like sprinkling poison over some frail sweet flower, withering its life and beauty. From that moment I feared all things, and surely I had reason.

' I had always been in the habit of keeping a journal—not one merely of dates and incidents, but a sketch likewise of thoughts and impressions, which I had felt from time

to time, and which it seemed a relief to pour
forth, though it were but in silent words
known only to myself. I had not opened it
for long, endeavouring rather to forget what
had interested me; and, fearing to awake
again feelings I had quieted and quelled;
but, a few mornings after the conversation I
have dilated on, I took out my journal and
began looking over it. As I read, the difference between past and present came pain-
fully home to me. I was deeply ruminating
over this, when Ellen called me. I left the
book, therefore, in my hurry, open on the
writing table, and ran hastily down stairs, leaving my door partly open. Ellen asked me to
finish a few bars of a song she was copying,
as Valerie was coming to drive with her. I
sat down and commenced it, while Ellen ran
to put her bonnet on. I heard Valerie
enter the house; but instead of coming into
the drawing-room, she went up stairs. They
could not have remained long there, for

I heard the carriage roll from the door almost immediately; and after finishing copying the song, I returned to my room; on entering it, I thought it had been foolish of me leaving my private journal thus exposed on my table, with the door partly open; yet, no one would come there, or, if they did, read what was marked private. No names were mentioned, nor even initials marked. I think I should never for an instant have dreamt of any one having done so, had it not been for finding Valerie's pocket handkerchief on the table: she then had been in my room, had looked at my journal, had read all my past life, or glanced at it sufficiently for me to be entirely in her power: the thought tortured me. I caught up the book, and locked it hastily in my desk. Before condemning Valerie, I would show the handkerchief, and watch her countenance well, while I did so. It seemed a lifetime till they came in; I could do no-

thing but pace up and down the room agitated and miserable; they remained out
late, and when they did come in, it was to
ask me to accompany them to the public
gardens, and hear the band, which I did.
Taking the handkerchief, I looked fully at
Valerie, and said—

" I found this in my room on the writing-
table."

A slight colour suffused her face; but
with great composure, she said—

" Thank you! I had forgotten it; your
door being partly open, and hearing Mr.
Churchill calling from below, I ran to your
window to answer him, and I suppose, left
my handkerchief by mistake."

I could not ask if she had read my writings,
but although it was perhaps wrong to judge
her, I felt thoroughly convinced she had
done so; the idea of my inmost thoughts
being known to one treacherous enough to
read them, and who would in all probability

divulge what she knew—and exaggerate what she had learned—proving perhaps to Ellen that I had deceived her in a thousand ways—made me feel ill at ease and unhappy. There were crowds of people walking to and fro, listening to the exquisite music ; and the whole scene was gay and pretty. Mr. Churchill, however, did not join us, and Valerie watched my countenance closely as she remarked this to Ellen ; and there was irony in the tone in which the words were uttered. Though not caring for Mr. Churchill, she was piqued at his having once cared for me, which, if she had read the journal, would have been plain to her ; or, if not, perhaps an observing and clever person might have noticed, when he had spoken of having my likeness taken, an interest in me, which, though generally carefully concealed, was still existing. Ellen remarked my loss of spirits, which she might well do, for my dread of Valerie's knowledge, and the use she might make of it, in causing

Ellen unhappiness, almost maddened me. A slight start Valerie made caused me to look up ; walking towards us was Louis Daubeney handsome as ever, only still more delicate in appearance than when I had last seen him ; the slight face still more pale and wasted, making the full and brilliant eyes appear larger, and with his finely-formed head and classical features, I thought, as he approached, I had never seen any one half so handsome.

Valerie could not conceal her delight ; her whole face glowed with pleasure, and with her eyes radiant and flashing with joy, she sprang forward to greet him ; she looked into his face, and the fond heart-rending glance with which he returned it, told me of his enduring but hopeless love for the woman, who had basely won his heart but to trample on and crush it. There again, face to face, did they stand together, unmindful of what others saw or thought concerning them.   She walked through the gardens, talking earnestly, whilst I followed with Ellen, who exclaimed—

" Really Mr. Daubeney is the handsomest man I have ever seen ; how pleased Valerie appears at meeting him again ! What a kind interest she takes in his welfare."

" She does take a very deep interest in him," I replied; " you know I saw them together at Wentworth Court."

" Yes !" answered Ellen, " and Valerie has told me how she always endeavoured to show him every kindness, even before the other guests, at her father's, knowing, gene-rally, what slights are shown to any one who may perhaps not be exactly in the same position as themselves; and I like it so much in her."

" If done from that motive, none would applaud her more than I should," I replied, " but I know to the contrary."

There was no answer made to this last

remark; in silence perhaps Ellen thought
of it, but I think she knew me well enough
to feel that I should not have uttered it
without reason; and as that might lower
Valerie in her eyes, she would not investigate
it.   Murmurs, as we passed through the
crowd, of wonder who that handsome fellow
was Lady Falconhurst had got with her,
were heard by us; if Valerie noticed them
or not I cannot tell, but she walked on, un-
heeding all but Louis Daubeney; speaking
but to him, and even the few favoured ones
who were generally by her side, were *now*
scarce seen, and utterly disregarded.   When
we reached the house she apologized to
Ellen for speaking exclusively to Mr.
Daubeney, but said there was so much business to talk about, she must forgive it.

" Farewell, darling," she said, " till to-
morrow; for a wonder we are to have a quiet
evening all to ourselves."

Wonderful, no doubt, when she had so

arranged it, and that Lord Falconhurst was
to go for a long ride with Mr. Churchill,
who was to have an early dinner with them,
which would enable them to take a longer
ride than usual, leaving Valerie to entertain
Louis Daubeney, whilst Ellen and I were left
tête-a-tête.

It was surprising, in Valerie's absence, how
much more pleasantly we talked together;
it seemed as though I were again in her old
home, sitting at her open window, gazing on
the declining sunset streaming its last rays
over the park, as we had done a few evenings
before her marriage.

CHAPTER III.

For some days after this the pictures seemed not thought of even. Mr. Daubeney joined in all the gaieties with Lord and Lady Falconhurst, and parties were even formed for his amusement. I wondered he liked thus to linger in the society of a woman, who, for mere worldly considerations, had cast him off; also that Lord Falconhurst liked the intimacy that existed between his wife and an unknown artist.

Edward Churchill again spoke of having my picture done, but I refused the idea of

it in so decided a manner, that he said no
more on the subject. Mr. Daubeney commenced Ellen's, and after hers was finished,
Valerie was to sit again for hers. The Falconhursts' house being larger than her own,
Ellen went each morning over there to a
large unfurnished room, where she sat with
Valerie, who talked or read to Ellen, while
she remained, looking very pretty and in-
animate. M. Daubeney had genius enough
to give her features the animation and feeling
she lacked ; by doing so, rendering it a very
lovely picture. I don't remember Mr.
Churchill once coming to see it, or appearing
to take the slightest interest in the matter.
When it was quite finished, and every one
was admiring it, he agreed that it was certainly
rather like, and a very pretty picture ; but
he did not remember ever having seen his
wife look like it; that Mr. Daubeney had
given a force and expression in the mouth
and eyes that unfortunately Ellen never

possessed.   I had thought the same, though
I had not said so.   I wondered what his
second picture of Valerie would be like ;
and whether Ellen would go each morning
and sit with her.   I heard her offer to do so,
and recollect well her friend's reply ; she
was so much obliged, but it rather distracted
her attention too much to have people talking to her, and she preferred being alone.
I fancied I knew why, and I wondered Ellen
never perceived how entirely these two were
wrapt up in each other ; how every glance
revealed their affection, and how in each
other's presence they seemed to forget all
else but their guilty and absorbing love.

From the commencement of that likeness
being taken, began a new scene of trouble
to me.   Valerie again, like some evil spirit
that is ever hovering near to fling black and
heavy shadows on our path, now, from a
slight but unfortunate occurrence, again
commenced torturing me, and estranging

those from me, who were the only protectors I
had now to turn to in a foreign land.   Away
from the few friends I possessed, and placed
in the trying and difficult position I had so
long struggled against, and from which I had
for two years absented myself, only now
promising any degree of peace or happiness.
Valerie again, with her baneful influence,
must come among us, robbing me of all I
cared to keep : not content till she had
flung me back again on the world, a friendless
unhappy girl.   She strove, as she had once
before done, to quell in me the ever-flowing
tide of hope and buoyancy that bears us on
in the spring of life, perhaps through troubled waters, but still on and on, to what we
fancy a sunny shore.   What though that
land is never reached ? though each dream
·of life prove but a shadow that eludes our
grasp, and leaves us weary mid the strife and
toil ? still let us hope and pray, still let the
first spring flowers be the heralds of brighter

things; and when Summer shall be gliding past us in the full splendour of her noon-day sun, and bearing away on her breezes the rich scent of her gorgeous flowers, let us think of the calm autumn days with peace! Woe be to those who make this beautiful world desolate and hateful; who make us doubt, at last, the truth of all things, and, trusting no one, fall back on our own resources with distorted feelings! Sad indeed is the heart, where no hope raises it above these evils; when, bent down under silent suffering, it closes mournfully to a living grave.

From such mere trifles do marked events arise, that I think I might have remained during my stay in Germany without suffering much from Valerie's influence or malice, if she had not been in a measure placed in my power by a slight circumstance. It was early one morning, that, as Ellen and I sat together, she asked, if I would run in to

Lady Falconhurst's, and ask her for the third volume of a book she was much interested in : I told her I would willingly go, but I knew that Valerie would not like being disturbed while sitting for her picture ; she had asked us not to go till after two o'clock.

" Well," answered Ellen, " just look for it on the drawing-room table ; and if it is not there, knock at the door of the painting-room, and ask her where it is."

It was with anything but a pleasurable feeling I complied with this request. I looked carefully on the table over the numerous books that lay scattered about ; but after a vain search, ascended the stairs to the room where Mr. Daubeney and Valerie were sitting. I knocked again and again, but all in vain ; it was evident they were not there, or they could not fail to hear my repeated efforts to make them do so : pausing, therefore, for an instant only, I opened the door, and moved towards the table : it was a

long room, scantily furnished, cold-looking,
and bare; but, in the deep recess of the
window, sat Louis Daubeney and Valerie, a
book of poems in one hand—the other
held hers, whilst her magnificent speaking
eyes rested fondly and lovingly on his face.
But Oh! the change that my presence
wrought on both! he, growing pale as death,
rose up hastily; while Valerie, with a
glance I shall never forget, advanced slowly
towards me, composed, still, as though she
was neither surprised nor annoyed. I told
her of Ellen having sent me in search of a
book and bidding me come to the painting-
room in quest of it.

"I knocked two or three times," I added,
"but the room being so large, it is doubtless
difficult to hear."

Valerie made no reply; but handing me
the book, turned to Mr. Daubeney, and
said:—

"If you are sufficiently rested, we will

resume the work ;" then looking at me, she rejoined :—

" I make him rest every now and then for he is too delicate to paint for any time together."

Seating herself in a graceful attitude, she bade me give her love to Ellen, and I quitted the room.

And this was Ellen's chosen friend, this woman with neither heart nor principle ! yet how could I prevent it ? would not my telling Ellen what I had just seen, involve me, perhaps, in much unhappiness ? and yet, should I allow one so weak in character, and young in years, to love and cherish such as Valerie ? love for Ellen, and fear for myself and all, made me waver as to what course I should pursue.

When I entered the drawing-room, Ellen instantly remarked that something must have happened, for I looked flushed and be-wildered.

" If I were to tell you, you would not believe it," I said.

" Not believe you !" answered Ellen, with a look of astonishment.

" Do you not know, Ellen, that when people's minds are biassed strongly on one side, how very difficult it is to move the impression they have formed to any other belief ?"

" Certainly," she answered ; " but what has that to do with what we are now talking of ? has Valerie said anything to annoy you ?"

" No, she said very little ; but it was her actions startled and surprised me."

" Why, was she not sitting to Mr. Daubeney for her picture ?" asked Ellen.

" Sitting with him she certainly was," I replied, " whilst he read to her, her hand clasped in his."

" Well, that was strange certainly, Inez," said Ellen, colouring violently.

" Not strange, if you knew her well."

" But do you mean to insinuate that Valerie cares for Louis Daubeney, Inez ?"

" I am certain she does."

Ellen looked grave and unhappy for some moments, remaining silent, till she suddenly asked :—

" Why do you think so ?"

Sitting down by Ellen, I told her of all I had witnessed at Wentworth Court; of my knowledge of what brought him to Germany ; and of the wrong yet strong attachment that I could plainly see still existed between them, warning Ellen against being so very intimate, and begging her gradually to let it drop, but not to do so suddenly.   Ellen cried, and said, " she was very sorry to do so, she had fancied if there had been anything really against Valerie, her husband would never have allowed her to become such a friend of hers.

" I do not say there is any guilt except

in their love for each other, which you admit to be wrong, but I know her to be without principle, and devoid of truth, two essential things I should require in a friend."

" You have often told me this," answered Ellen, " and I do not doubt your word, but I cannot see it ; to me she appears all goodness and fascination : her manner is gentle and affectionate; her conversation clever and amusing ; and to give up her friendship will cost me much ; but if best to do it, it shall be done."

" I am sorry to pain you," I replied, kissing her ; " judge for yourself, dear Ellen ; act for yourself; my words were not meant to give you sorrow, but to save you from it ; let them therefore not weigh upon you, and forgive my having spoken them."

But at this moment the door opened, and Valerie entered. As she entered I left them together. It seemed an unfortunate moment for her to have come ; yet, I knew her motive

for doing so : she wished to find out from
Ellen's manner if I had told her anything of
what I had just witnessed ; and no doubt
the sign of tears on Ellen's face, and her
manner altogether, would prove this was
the case, and I wondered what the result of
this visit would be. Valerie did not stay
long, and when I heard her close the door
I ran down to ask Ellen what had passed.

"Very little," she replied ; "Valerie
merely ran in to ask us all there this evening.
She enquired if I had heard any distressing
news, for I looked quite melancholy. I told
her, nothing of consequence. She appeared
quite satisfied, and went away soon after. I
know not how to act towards her," continued
Ellen, sadly ; "if I grow cold in manner
she will enquire the cause, and much mischief may ensue from it ; yet, if she is really
the heartless flirt you describe, I know
Edward would not like me to be so very intimate with her as I have hitherto been ; it

is difficult to know what to do in a case of
this sort."

"Nothing more so," I replied; "and if
I were in your place I should do nothing
rashly or without thought; if you could do
her any good, or influence her in any way to
act rightly, I should be the last person to
induce you to give up her friendship : it was
for your own self I spoke."

"I know it," answered Ellen, gently,
"but let us both watch them this evening."

"You might watch them a whole evening,
or many months," I replied, "and see
nothing : it was a mere chance made me
know of their affection for each other ; you
see Lord Falconhurst is as ignorant as you
were this morning ; and he is her husband."

"But perhaps he is a very unobserving
person, Inez ; now I am not ; I see things
very quickly."

I did not contradict her, but I think it
proved what I had often thought, how little

people know of their own characters. My
only dread was now, that Valerie would more
than ever fear my remaining with Ellen ; my
influence over her ; my divulging what she
was well aware I knew ; and her aim would
be, I felt certain, to separate us. I had been
more than six weeks in Germany, and had
enjoyed them ; I feared that the remainder
of my visit would be passed in a different
and, in all probability, a very unhappy manner. I wondered why fate had again thrown
Valerie with me ; I lost all my cheerfulness
as I thought of her, and of the misery she
would, I feared, bring on us both.

There had been nothing in Valerie's
manner to convince Ellen of the truth of
what I had told her during the evening we
spent at the Falconhursts : indeed Valerie
was more than usually attentive to her husband. With her now quiet manner, simple
dress, and apparent disregard of self, it would
have been difficult for the closest observer to

have detected the real character through this mask of virtue. I had been greatly amused at a young clergyman, whom I met there, and recognized as one of the curates we had seen a good deal of whilst at Mrs. Harley's. He came up to me towards the end of the evening, and after asking how I liked what I had seen of Germany, said—

" Are you staying with your cousin ?"

I told him, no, but I saw her every day as she was an intimate friend of Mrs. Churchill's.

" I am delighted to have the pleasure of renewing my acquaintance with her," he said. " She is certainly a charming person."

Not being able to agree with all this, I merely replied—

" She is clever, and very handsome."

" Yes !" he replied ; " and yet how perfectly indifferent she is to her beauty ; how little she thinks of or values it. I like her simplicity of dress, too ; it seems to suit her mind, which is as beautiful as her face ; and though she is clever, she is simple-minded and free from all affectation ; she has such sound good principles : I only wish I possessed such a treasure in my parish, instead of the gay fashionable young woman who has lately married the lord of the manor ; how much good might be done among the poor, and the services of the church how kept up, if such a woman as your cousin, Lady Falconhurst, was there to interest herself about them."

I could scarcely repress a smile as I listened to this folly ; but I glanced at Valerie, who was sitting at the other end of the room. She was certainly looking very lovely, her plain white muslin dress was high, drawn simply round her long fair throat; her only ornament a diamond chain and cross ; her sunny hair waving off her clear, almost transparent face, and only confined by a few leaves of the Virginian creeper.

" Yes, she is very lovely," I said aloud, almost forgetting the presence of my friend, the curate, whose eyes were feasting on the beauty of the high-principled, amiable Valerie. I turned away, and close behind me sat Edward Churchill ; he evidently had heard our conversation, for as the young clergyman moved on to where Valerie was sitting, he drew his chair near, and said—

" *Great* judge of character, that man."

I only smiled.

" He and Ellen are equally clever at reading the human heart," he continued ; " don't you think so ?"

" They are blind, and therefore cannot be blamed; it is only those who know better, and yet pay the same homage, that I can find fault with."

" She is a beautiful woman, and would flirt with any one who liked to flirt with her ; but, Inez, why should *you* care ?"

" For Ellen's sake," I answered ; " Valerie is no safe companion for her, I well know."

After a silence of some moments, he said—

" It is all alike to me ; weary of everything, I snatch at the amusement each affords, vain and unprofitable as they all are. We must only hope and pray that the toil and weariness may soon cease ; annihilation will bring rest."

" The soul never rests," I said.

" It may rest awhile from torturing thoughts that burn into it, till in this world it becomes a hell."

" Try rather," I said, in a low tone of voice, " to obtain peace on earth, and then you may hope for it hereafter."

" Then black, indeed, must my future be," he answered : " *peace !*" The last word was uttered almost inaudibly, but the closely compressed quivering lip seemed powerless to utter more.

I turned from him, but not before Valerie's quick glance had rested with malicious scrutiny on both. Ellen was beside her, but walking towards her husband, I heard her say " Edward, I am sure you are ill, you look so strange and pale ; does he not, Inez ?"

" He looks pale and tired : I suppose it is time to be going."

" Yes, come along," he said, laughing ; " you will both frighten me into a fit if I remain here, with your dismal description of my appearance."

He walked away to where Valerie and several others were sitting, while Ellen said :

" What was Edward talking about ?"

" He was speaking of the cares of life, and of what we might hope another exist-ence would be ; rather a serious conversation for a party."

" Very !" she answered, sighing. " How strange of him !"

She wished Valerie good night, who, with Mr. Daubeney on one side of her, and the curate on the other, looked perfectly happy.

CHAPTER IV.

ALTHOUGH Ellen had not in any way changed in her manner towards Valerie, I noticed that she was not so pressing for her to come and sit with us each day as she had hitherto been, before I told her of the scene in the painting room. I knew that it gave Ellen some pain to do this; but a feeling that she was acting rightly, made her firm to the promise she had given me of endeavouring by degrees to break an intimacy that might lead to unpleasant results.

Valerie saw it also with her usual quickness; and angry at the change, and fearful
of the consequences, she would sometimes
look at me with an expression of determined
revenge, that I felt she would, sooner or
later, put into execution. If she had, as I
feared, glanced over my journal, much would
be revealed that she might construe which
way she pleased; and how much suffering
might arise from one careless act! The
very sight of Valerie made me tremble. I
never heard her enter the house without a
strange dread overwhelming me; and as I
saw gradually Ellen's manner towards her
grow more reserved, approaching even to
coldness, I felt that sooner or later some
explanation would be asked, and perhaps
granted.

———— ————

A world of time and thought has passed
since then, joy, pain, death, and agony of
heart, sweeping past with the full tide of
life; yet, in lingering on the past, what pain

was so bitter as I felt *then* ? How clearly I remember it, seeming, as I now write, to come
back with even stronger force, now that, in
calm contemplation, I can feel what it has
left me—not wretched or heart-broken, not
angry and bitter, or, perhaps, worse still,
grown hard, with the world's brand of indifference stamped on me : like one recovered
from some torturing illness, which had well-
nigh deprived the sufferer of life and strength,
yet from which he rises better and stronger
in heart—so did I feel, when, having passed
through the fiery ordeal of one of life's
hardest punishments, I stood forth alone to
begin life.—I say *begin ;* for, still so young
in years, there was, and perhaps is still in
store, many a weary hour to come—many
a heart-struggle untold, to be kept under in
silent agony ; yet, with a firmer will, a calmer
feeling to help me on hopefully and endur-
ingly to the end.   Vividly each moment
comes before me.   I remember the first

change in Ellen Churchill's manner, as if it were but an hour ago that the scene I am about to describe passed before me. I have said that a slight estrangement had sprung up between Ellen and my cousin Valerie. I watched it for days with anxiety and suspense, expecting the crisis, which came soon enough. It was one day, which I had gone to spend with a friend of Ellen's who had often pressed me to do so, that Valerie proposed to come to Ellen and bring her work. Ellen agreed to it; but there was no warmth of manner in the acceptance of the offer made. I noticed this particularly, and wondered if she had seen anything in Valerie's manner to Mr. Daubeney that had at last made her feel the truth of what I had said. It was late in the evening when I came home. The servant informed me, that Lady Falconhurst had gone, and that Mrs. Churchill was not at all well, had gone to bed, and did not wish to be disturbed. I

waited anxiously till I heard Edward
Churchill come in, when I asked him if he
had seen Ellen, telling him what the servant
had said. He answered that he had not, but
would do so immediately, and come and let
me know how she was. More than an hour
passed; yet he did not come. I waited
anxiously, fearing that Ellen was very ill;
at last he entered the drawing-room and
said—

" Inez, I cannot make out what is the
matter with Ellen; she would scarcely turn
and speak to me; traces of tears are on her
face, and her whole frame is trembling violently. I have sent for the doctor, for I am
sure she is very ill."

" Let me go to her," I exclaimed, and
without waiting a reply, I ran hastily to her
room; it was almost dark, the blinds were
down, and the thick curtains also drawn
round the bed where Ellen lay. Pale as a
ghost she looked as she turned towards

me when I spoke, for a moment ; then, hiding her face in her trembling hands, she
made no reply to my inquiry for her.
Annoyed at her strange manner, I had
scarcely power to speak for some moments.

"Ellen !" I at last exclaimed, " what has
happened ? You are surely very ill ?"

" I shall be soon better," she said at last.
" I only wish to be alone ; let no one come
near me."

I did not answer ; I remained sitting by
her bed-side in silence, till Mr. Churchill
and the doctor entered. What a cold feeling of horror crept over me as I left the
room ! Ellen's state, I knew, could proceed
only from great mental suffering ; and knowing that Valerie had spent the day with her
alone, I had not the slightest doubt, in my
own mind, of what had passed between
them. All that I had feared and foreseen
for long, had now reached this unhappy
crisis. Vexed, miserable, and sick at heart, I

flung myself on my bed, and wept. Hearing
from the servant that Mrs. Churchill was a
little easier, I endeavoured to sleep; but
my aching eyes were not closed the whole
of that anxious and ill-fated night. When
I entered the breakfast room the next morning, Edward Churchill was there alone.

" What a pale, care-worn face, Inez !"
he said, looking up at me from his book;
" why, what is the matter with you all?
Ellen has done nothing but faint and tremble
all night ; and you look as if you were going
to follow her example."

" I have had no sleep," I answered;
" Ellen seeming so ill alarmed me. What
does the doctor think of her ?"

" He says she has been greatly agitated
in some way, and that there is something on
her mind ; he instantly gave her composing
draughts, which, I am thankful to say, at
last sent her to sleep; but as I am anxious
about her, I should like you, Inez, to go to

her presently, and ask her what is the matter."

I would willingly have told my fears to Mr. Churchill regarding Valerie; but, fearing lest it should make matters worse, I only answered, that I would go instantly, and endeavour to find out from Ellen what had caused her sudden illness. I did so. She was sitting near her window, leaning her face down as if deep in thought, never turning to me as I approached.

" Ellen," I said, " I trust you are better; you have been the cause of great anxiety to your husband and me."

" *Great*, I should imagine," she answered, her generally gentle expression assuming a hard cold look.

" Do you not believe it, then?" I asked.

" I believe in nothing," she answered. " I have no faith left in any earthly thing— why should I?"

" Why should you *not*?" I said, looking

calmly and steadfastly in her face ; " or rather why thus suddenly waken to this knowledge?"

" It matters not how or why—miserable I am, and must ever be," she said. " *You* know it," she continued angrily, " you, who from first to last have cruelly deceived me." She sobbed violently.

" I never deceived you, Ellen ; you have deceived yourself ; yet, happy in your ignorance, might you have enjoyed life's richest blessings, had not one with subtle treachery robbed you of it."

" Yes, this has always been your aim and object," she replied, " to blind me by your artifice ; but I credit it no longer. To hide your own deceit, you would still endeavour to estrange me from one who has proved my best friend, by telling me the truth, and the secret of Edward's love for you which you returned. Oh," she continued, with a burst of grief, " what a deluded, wretched girl I have been for long ! Go ; I would not, cannot be unkind to you, though you have robbed me of all that made my life sweet!"

I did not answer Ellen; I could not speak! All my sacrifice of self, all my agony of heart, rushed upon me, and a sudden darkness overwhelmed me; there seemed no light in earth or in heaven; yet, I stood calm and cold, silent, yet despairing. I pleaded nothing then; I did not vindicate myself. There are moments in life when words are vain, when consolation is useless, when hope is dead. So it was with me, as I gently moved from the room. I sought Mr. Churchill, and told him all I had heard from Ellen. Pale, agitated, and angry, he listened, till, rising up with flashing eyes, he said—

" I will go to her, and tell her all the truth. Inez, you who have acted rightly, who have sacrificed your own life's joy for her, do you think *she* is thus to ill-treat and trample on you? No; were you less dear

to me ; were you selfish instead of generous ;
even then this should not be ; so I will go
and tell her so."

" Pray do not," I said, laying my hand
on his arm to prevent his leaving the room ;
" in Ellen's present state, she would not
listen calmly, or believe anything. When
people's minds are agitated strangely, and
strongly biassed, it is long before they can
listen to reason ; when she is calm and
better, tell her ; she is generous, therefore
will be forgiving. Let us first find out what
Lady Falconhurst has told her."

" But how," interrupted Mr. Churchill,
" could she have known all this ? If I have,
alas ! ever betrayed that I once loved you,
surely your quiet manner and utter disregard
of me must have proved that you had no
feeling in the matter."

I hesitated for an instant ; then told him
my fears regarding the journal that had lain
open on the table, and of finding Valerie's

handkerchief close to it; of her confusion on my giving it to her, and of my thorough conviction that she would not hesitate a moment reading its contents. In a few words I revealed to him all I had known and seen of Valerie's conduct, not only towards myself, but to Mr. Daubeney, and of my having warned Ellen against allowing an intimacy and affection to spring up between them, that would lead to painful results.

" You have acted wisely," he said : " fool —madman, that I have been ! first, for being persuaded into marrying a weak, soulless girl; and then for permitting an intimacy to exist between her and one whom I knew to be a dreadful flirt, but whose cleverness and beauty amused and pleased me ! Inez," he continued, solemnly, taking my hand in his, " my life for the last two years has been any-thing but good or profitable. Unhappy at heart, I sought in gaiety and dissipation to

quell for ever the deepest feeling of my life.
I have succeeded—succeeded so far, that
now I can look on you calmly, think of you
as of one dead to me indeed for ever. Yet,
still with an interest that will not end even
with life, I cannot, however, pause and
think—I cannot rest. Ah! in your calm
eyes I read your thoughts. You are blam-
ing me for this. I know what you would
say—what consolation you would offer; *that*
may come in time, but a fiery ordeal must
be passed before; tell me more of this
Valerie. Why is she treacherous to you?
—why does she hate you?"

I then related fully, from my first acquaintance with my cousin up to the
present time, of my astonishment at finding
Ellen in such close companionship with one
so unworthy as Valerie; of my entreaties
that she would relinquish the friendship,
and of my dread of that influence over a

mind like Ellen's, which I knew that Valerie would obtain.

" Yes," he answered, musingly, " I should not have allowed it; liking Lady Falconhurst's talents and beauty, I rather encouraged Ellen in making her acquaintance, forgetting that, though I could see plainly the true character of such a woman, and not trust too much to her, Ellen, with her usual want of discernment and tact, would rush too hastily into a friendship I might repent of hereafter. By my folly, Inez, you see what I have brought upon you."

" I must leave you, and soon," I answered, calmly. " Again must I go forth alone, and with this desolate feeling, that my having endeavoured to do right, though a comfort to my own heart, has still brought sorrow to those I love."

As I said these words, I leant down and buried my aching head among the cushions of the sofa, to hide from him the bitter burning tears that would fall.

" Look up, Inez—look at me, my poor heart-broken Inez, and read in my eyes if I could ever doubt you, or be unkind to you."

I could not look up ; shuddering, I fell in a deep swoon at his feet ; and all thought, all misery, all memory, had vanished ——.

Then there comes a time to my remembrance, more torturing still—a time when I was recovering from an attack of fever that lasted some weeks after I had fallen at Mr. Churchill's feet like one dead, when Ellen came and nursed me, and was kind and gentle, too ; but on her face a world of pain was settled, and when she smiled, it was no longer sweet and sunny. With a fold of reserve, like a dense cloud separating us, her eyes averted from my glance ; she did her duty, and no more. Oh ! time of agony and fear ! dreading to speak of what was ever present, shrinking from explanation, till at last speech seemed gone, and my ideas stiffened and congealed like ice, which no human touch could thaw! Oh! heart-agony, to see distrust spring up between man and wife, and know that I had caused it! Sickening to witness her young face turned from his calm and statue-like, and as cold! with no expression but of pain ever gleaming from her eyes!—to hear her answer coldly, or, when he called her to him, walk with a cold, proud step to him she loved —like one who chose still to obey him, though he loved her not! All this, and more than I could write, was ever present to me. I need not dilate upon its wretchedness; rather would I hasten to our parting, bitter as that was too, than linger on this time of misery. Mr. Churchill had quarrelled with Valerie, and forbade Ellen to see much of her. I guessed this would be the case, and the disturbance it would cause in the two families. I had not seen Valerie since, owing to my illness; but I knew that her anger and revenge would know no bounds. I knew that Ellen saw her whenever she could manage it, that she still believed in and cared for her.

Lord Falconhurst had been away on a visit during this painful time, but was expected home daily. On his return, Valerie would of course tell her own plausible story, be listened to and believed by him : he of course would take up the quarrel, would seek explanation of Mr. Churchill, and then what it might end in made me tremble to think of. Oh! with what a tortured heart did I wait the result of an interview between them ! with what agonised feeling did I one evening, as we three sat silent together, hear Lady Falconhurst announced! She came in proudly with a firm and bold step, her eyes severe and haughty, her face flushed, her full lips pallid with rage.

" I come here to vindicate myself," she said, looking round proudly, with the air of an empress, " to vindicate myself from false and cruel accusations. Who dares to doubt my word here? who dares to come forward and tell me so?"

Ellen sat trembling, not moving, only white as her dress, and shaking with agony. Weak as I was from my recent illness, I looked her fully in the face, though for a few moments I did not speak, for Mr. Churchill answered thus :—

" Who was it, Lady Falconhurst, that first came and made division here?—who poured into my wife's ear things that never should have been uttered, because they never should have been known? I ask you this in answer to your proud questioning, and also how you gained the knowledge you have so cruelly imparted? Not from *me*— not from Miss Wentworth, whose manner is calm and pure as an angel's—not from

Ellen, who, till you came among us, was
free and happy as a child. Yes, stand there
with that resolute haughty look and determined will; but let us hear your vindi-
cation of self, since you have come to
prove it."

Edward Churchill had said this very
calmly; but I knew his expression well
enough to feel that he was very angry.
Ellen, with a sudden burst of grief, entreated that no more might be said on the
subject, while Valerie answered—

" No more said upon the subject! Do
you, then, think I am to be thus treated?
But never mind; Lord Falconhurst comes
home to-night, and he shall settle it."

At these words, Ellen, who had remained
weeping at the other end of the room,
made one spring forward—a shrill cry of
agony burst from her lips, and falling on
her knees before Valerie, she cried—

" Oh, no, no, not *that*; I could not bear

it; for my sake, have mercy. Edward is *all*
to me. Oh! God! if I *lost him!* Kill me
—do what you will with me, but spare
Edward! Oh! save him!"

She looked as she spoke like one bereft of
reason, her ghastly face streaming with
tears, her eyes starting wildly in her agony,
her hair flung back, and her pale lips quivering; powerless, weak, and despairing as
she was, Mr. Churchill took her quietly in
his arms, and bore her from the room. I
heard her sobs echoing through the hall, as
he carried her up stairs. Alone with Valerie,
who had not moved, and on whose face a
devilish expression rested, I said—

"Valerie, is it not sufficient that you
have succeeded well in torturing me since I
first knew you, that you now must come
here and blast Ellen's happiness for life?"

As I glanced up at her, as she confronted
me, white with anger, she replied—

"Do you think *you* will conquer? that

your words will be believed before *mine;*
think of *your* position in life, and then on
mine. You," she added, contemptuously,
" you, alike contemptible and false! Ask
me how I read your secret, and I will tell
you; I read it in your every look and tone.
Do you think because Edward Churchill
has an innocent unsuspecting wife, that
your vile conduct can remain unnoticed? I
wonder you can look thus calmly into my
face : but see, you cannot answer me ; shame
makes you silent at least."

It was so difficult to keep calm, or to still
the rising anger of my heart, at the insults
just heaped on me! Yet, knowing how much
more power one has to speak when calm,
than when agitated by passion, I crushed
mine down, and answered with quiet composure. I told her that rank or power
could not prevail against truth ; that ere
she cast the stone at others she had best
reflect on her own conduct ; what it had

been for some time past, what she was feeling at the present moment.

Then, with proud and flashing eyes, she asked me what I meant; what I dared to insinuate against her, pure as she was, loving her husband as she did.   She guessed to whom I alluded ; and cruel and base it was of me to construe a real act of charity to a poor orphan, who, but for her, might be starving, into any motive but that of goodness.   I told her I was not her judge ; her course of conduct could not signify to me ; I knew little of her, wished to know still less ; I should not linger there to be insulted by her.   And, so saying, I left the room ; though her voice, angry, thrilling, and agitated, implored me to come back. As I glanced at her face, on leaving, there was an agonized expression of fear and of dismay, as well as of rage, disturbing her beautiful features.

I met Edward Churchill on the staircase ;

he beckoned me to the room where Ellen often sat of a morning, and with more agitation in his manner than I had noticed for long, he said—

"Whatever we do, or whatever happens in consequence of that woman Valerie's conduct, *Ellen* must be kept in the dark about it; I believe that any further misery or excitement about it would kill her."

"Certainly," I answered; "I was now on my way to her, to see if in any degree I could obliterate the impression Valerie has made her form of me, or help to soothe her by any means in my power."

"I think just now, Inez, nothing you or I could say would be felt or even believed by Ellen; Lady Falconhurst has gained, for a time, *that* power which her artificial kind of cleverness impresses on a mind like Ellen's, imaginative, yet weak and powerless; it was *my* mistake to let this intimacy gain ground. I fear much that is disagreeable

will result from it; but, however *that* may
be, excepting for Ellen's sake I do not dread
that silly husband of Lady Falconhurst's."

" Yet I trust," I replied, looking up with
some fear, " that nothing serious will occur;
do you think Valerie will dare tell him
what has passed? don't you think, by doing
so, she would dread detection?"

" She is quite clever enough to deceive
him," answered Edward, smiling; " do you
think that any one but a fool would have
allowed that young Daubeney to sit all day
with her in that painting-room, or not have
perceived what exists between them? it
does not escape the observation of others,
for within the last few days several men
have remarked it to me, and laughingly
said, they wondered what that donkey of a
husband was about, to let that beautiful
young wife of his be so intimate with the
handsomest fellow they had ever come
across."

" I felt assured," I answered, " that people would in time find out what has been evident to me for so long."

" I pity poor Daubeney," said Edward ; " he is not a bad youth at all; and, with his talent and beauty, might have made a path for himself through life, had he not been led away, as so many unfortunate men are, by an artful and designing woman : of course she does not care one straw about him; it is mere vanity, for she has *no* feeling."

" Selfish, of course, it is," I replied, " yet I believe Louis Daubeney is the only being who has ever touched her heart."

" I never found out that she possessed one," he answered; " when I have, I shall perhaps know better where it is centered. Go to Ellen now, and come to me in the evening. I am going out, and shall not be home to dinner."

He left, and, entering Ellen's room, I sat

reading by her side, for she had fallen asleep; sleep! that greatest blessing we possess, when, at least for some hours, rest comes to the thinking soul, as dew softens the parched and weary flowers, folding their leaves through the long night in sleep, and though with morning comes the toil and heat, we know that evening will bring rest again. Where were all the stormy passions that had agitated Ellen's breast? where was the gnawing pain that ate into her heart and poisoned her existence?—all alike hushed and still; on her young fair face rested no shadow of pain, calm as a child's, resting serenely on her pillow; all thought, misery, and care were banished in sleep.

As I sat watching her, visions of the past rose up before me, till memory became a torture instead of a blessing, and its sharp pain pierced me through and through. No sleep had visited my weary and swollen eyes; weak from recent illness, with nothing cheerful to dwell upon, and with the irreparable loss of a heart that had once trusted in and loved me, *now* changed and embittered. what had I to bid me *hope*? what should I do in the future? whither turn for justice or for truth? Could worldly pleasure give me comfort? it might stifle for awhile my grief; but should I not be clutching at a shadow that would elude my grasp, and make me fall back again on my own resources, with self-contempt embittering my every action, till I scorned my own self-abasement?— Would human affection satisfy and give me joy? but *it* might also turn aside, at the slightest provocation or fancy, and leave me again alone, with the dreary conviction, that having given my life's best feeling, my heart's tenderest love, it might be all thrust back in cold asperity on my crushed and broken spirit. I thought thus as I sat alone that dreary evening, and reflected thus, speaking to my own concience in words like

these :   Why do you linger thus unoccupied,
brooding over dismal thoughts, till your mind
becomes weak, as your frame is now suffering
and trembling ? have you no pride or power ·
to help yourself that you sit weeping over
what cannot be altered? Is it necessary, because one friend has changed, owing to false
and base calumny being whispered, and for a
time believed in, that all friends should prove
faithless ? or, if the one deep passion of your
life be flung from you of your own free will,
and that sacrifice of self, instead of bringing
a blessing, brings a curse, why should you
doubt that in many hearts beats a holy and a
true love ? or why question God's providence?
If your future be as you have pictured it,
vain, hopeless, dark, have you not a Father in heaven who cares for you, and pities
you ? With this thought, the sun for a
moment streamed into the room : it seemed
to bid me take comfort; and falling on my
knees beside Ellen, who still lay sleeping,

I breathed a supplication for pardon and for peace.   It is necessary, I thought, as I rose, cheered and hopeful, to *act*, not to think ; to journey on with a brave heart, not linger idly by the way, with no strength of purpose, no power of thought. Seeing Ellen's writing-case on the table, I drew forth a sheet of paper, and commenced writing her a letter. Many tears blotted the closely-written pages, tears of real sorrow, as I wrote of much that had cost me days and months of pain.   Yet, I could *write* what I could not have *spoken ;* and whether it were believed or not, I felt that I was performing a painful duty, in acquainting one whom I still loved with much that might pain her ; though I did not reveal all I had borne and sacrificed for her sake in quiet endurance.

I waited with Ellen till I heard her hus-band's step approach ; she started from her sleep at the sound ; and I, wishing to leave them together, quitted the room with the letter

E 2

in my hand.   On reaching my apartment, I
commenced a letter to an aunt of mine, a
Mrs. Hetherington, who had lately come
from India, and who had written twice to me
pressing me to stay with her as long as I
liked in her new home in Hampshire.   She
was alone, and would be glad of a companion ; and as I needed a kind friend and
a home, I wrote, thankfully accepting her
invitation. Nothing that Edward Churchill
might say should change this resolve ; if I
had been firm at the first, and had refused
this second invitation of his and Ellen's to
visit them, kind and pressing as it had been,
how much that now might take months,
even years, to rectify, might have been
spared, because never known !

CHAPTER V.

ELLEN appeared better the next day; and when she came among us again, though her manner was more thoughtful and saddened, it had regained its usual gentleness. It seemed to me as if she was endeavouring to make up, by kindness of manner, for what had passed, though her feelings had not changed in consequence. I had determined on not giving her my letter till I parted from her; a long parting it would be in all human probability. Never again would I disturb her peace—never again cause dissension between two people who, notwithstanding all I had borne from them, were still very dear to me. Oh! that I could have left Ellen with the thought, that though she believed me false, I was and would ever prove truer to her than the friend who maligned me, and who had no love or sincerity in her heart, either for Ellen, or any other human being, save the affection she felt for Louis Daubeney. Time would prove all things. There might come a period when Ellen, with her true and generous heart, would bid me come to her once more, leaving the forgotten past behind, only remembering me as she loved me first; therefore, hope on, crushed and bleeding heart—your trial is hard now, and your pain is acute; but there will come a time of change and rest, even though many weary years of suffering may be still in store for you. Commence to live in real earnest, droop not at every blast that threatens to

destroy—be earnest, active, hopeful; you
have youth, freshness, and energy—will not
these satisfy you? Thoughts like these
were written in my journal—that journal
which had cost me so much pain; yet, there
has always seemed a comfort to pour forth
one's thoughts on paper, rather than let
them lie for ever buried deep, unuttered,
till they burn into the heart like fire. Lady
Falconhurst did not appear for two days.
What mischief she might be concocting in
her own mind, I know not; but as Lord
Falconhurst had come, and not sought any
explanation of Edward Churchill, it had
turned out most likely, as I had fancied,
that not one single word of this quarrel had
been mentioned to her husband; she would,
of course, naturally fear discovery of her
own treacherous conduct if it were closely
investigated; and Valerie was much too
clever to run any risk of that sort, at a time
when she was at the height of enjoyment,

and most feared detection. Ellen made no comment on her absence; she must have noted it in her own mind, but seemed resolved not to speak of it. I never alluded to the subject; indeed, I wished, for the few days I remained, to let no further cause of dissension arise between us. Valerie had already done so much towards the estrangement that existed between us, and would, if in her power, do still more, that I resolved in my own mind to let the matter rest, determining, that when I parted from Ellen, I would place a long and explanatory letter in her hands : if she believed it, she would of course write, and beg that all the past might be forgotten; if, on the contrary, Valerie was believed, and my words and conduct not credited, I should but have done my duty in giving her the choice between us. Blinded as she now was, there might come a time when Valerie would be seen in her true character, and my words be remembered. The veil that had so long hidden the evil might be drawn aside. When the time drew near for my departure, I acquainted Ellen with it. She started and coloured deeply, saying—

" Oh, Inez, do not leave us ! We still hope that you will stay."

She endeavoured to say this as of old, and I felt that her heart smote her for the languid way in which the request was uttered ; not raising her eyes from her work, she seemed to wait for my reply. I thanked her sincerely, not only for her invitation, but for much kindness. I told her at the same time that Mrs. Hetherington had so urged me to come to her, that I could no longer refuse : she was lonely and an invalid ; moreover, almost my only relation who had come forward to befriend me ; therefore I could not refuse her request, at a time when she needed a companion. Ellen did not answer ; I fancied that a few tears fell from her eyelids on her work, though she still remained silent. Mine were fast gathering to my eyes, and not venturing to speak lest my feelings should overpower me, I rose quickly, and quitted the room.

It was the day following this conversation, that Edward Churchill proposed that we should take a long ride to some woods about ten miles off, in the middle of which was an old chateau. We had heard much of its beauty, and had often thought of going there. As I was so soon to leave, we agreed to go that afternoon. I had seen little of the surrounding country, and was, therefore, glad of the opportunity. The day was fine, and promised much pleasure. Ellen, too, appeared in better spirits. Edward was also very pleasant: the exercise seemed to have a good influence upon us; and the restraint under which we had lived for so long, disappeared.

A promise of coming brightness lightened

my heart from its load of anxiety: the air, clear, fresh, and bracing, was likely to have this effect on a frame weakened by illness and grief; and we all talked cheerfully as we rode together.

The grand pine forests rose dark and thick, only lightened, here and there, by gleams of sunshine; it seemed a contrast to the brightness we had left behind; yet, so beautiful in its dark grandeur, that, for a moment, in its solemn stillness, it seemed to bid us be dark, gloomy, and silent, ere we entered its mysterious precincts. My thoughts wandered back to the damp dark wood, the deep pool of water, the rude bench on which two names were carved, and the flash that followed the golden ring flung into its closing waters: thinking still on this, my eyes met Edward Churchill's, and the deep glance of his revealed that his thoughts were dwelling on the same thing; he rode off in a quick canter; Ellen and I

followed, our speed preventing further conversation, which relieved my mind thus disturbed by memories of the past.

We entered these dark woods at last: in
the thickest part rose the turrets of the old
chateau, relieving the gloom ; a gay flower-
garden was spread before the low stone wall
that skirted the broad path beneath the
deep-set windows ; the sighing of the pine-
trees fell like the sound of distant waters on
my senses, as they were stirred by the
passing breeze.

The Baron de Montfort's family being
away, we were at liberty to see all that was
worth seeing: we heard the bell resound
through and through, till the echoes were
startling in the midst of so grave-like a stillness. The old housekeeper came to the
door ; she eyed us with much curiosity and
surprise ; Ellen begged to be allowed to see
the old castle, and to explore the garden
and woods ; the old woman nodded her

head in assent, and then, with her ponderous keys by her side, she bade us follow
her; on, through dark halls, corridors, and
winding passages we passed: handsome
furniture lay scattered about; there seemed
no notion of order or elegance; oak tables,
chairs and sofas, dark and gloomy-looking,
were scantily furnishing the large cold
rooms, looking as if no human hands ever
touched or handled them—certainly no
woman's; no carpets, either, or curtains, to
enliven their solemn aspect. I remarked
this to the old woman, who answered—

" It's good enough and elegant enough
for them that lives in it; I'll take no
trouble to make it otherwise than what it is."

Edward Churchill and Ellen having
lingered in a picture-gallery, I had followed
the sulky old woman on and on, without
thinking much what I was about; but, at
these strange words, I answered—

" Of what does the family consist? is the
Baroness alive?"

" She has lain in her grave these many years," she replied with the same dogged air; " and the Baron and Miss Clara seldom enter their home:" she had seemed on the point of uttering something harsh, from the expression of her face; but turning round, said—

" There are some private sitting-rooms; perhaps you don't care for them; they are small and plainly furnished."

" I should like to see them," I answered; and she opened a door from the hall, and we entered a narrow passage with doors on either side. I noticed a drawing-room scantily furnished like the rest, but looking more civilized, from there being an old grand piano at the end of it, and a harp, whose strings were almost all broken, but looking, as if, *once*, light fingers might have swept the chords in tones sweet and thrilling: a heap of old music lay beside it, and as I stooped to examine it, the name of Beatrice

de Montford was written, much faded by
time and dust, but still plainly marked upon
each piece of music, in a delicate and beautiful hand.   I wished much to enquire who
Beatrice might be, whether a daughter of
the Baron's, or not ; but fearing I might be
deemed too inquisitive, by asking so many
questions, and seeing my guide was not
likely or willing to impart anything, I left
the room in silence.   I wandered on to one
smaller but more cheerful-looking than any
I had yet seen.   I saw old frame-works
looking more like a room inhabited by
ladies, and a small but handsome table on
which books lay scattered, and albums and
sketch-books, with half-finished sketches of
the surrounding scenery, some of which I
recognised.   I had hastily glanced on these,
in passing by the table ; but, on looking up,
perceived the housekeeper's scrutinizing
glance resting on me.

"Are these Miss Clara's sketches?" I

enquired, somewhat confused at having taken this liberty.

" No, she does not draw," was the only answer to my question. " This room," she said, " opens into a bed-room, and on to some others forming a suite of rooms. You can see them if you like."

I walked by her in total silence. Whether or not the old castle had tinged my imagination, from its gloom and quaintness, I could not tell; but I was suddenly impressed with an idea that the family which inhabited it was wrapt in some mysterious romance that I could never fathom. Thinking of this, my eyes rested on two pictures, one seeming to look straight down on me, the other turned with its face to the wall. Handsome and peculiar-looking was the one I now gazed at, of a girl, young, light-complexioned, with fair hair and finely-marked features, but eyes of nut brown, and strongly-marked eyebrows : beautiful as

it struck me to be, the more I looked at it,
the less I liked it. There was an expression
in the face of dissatisfaction and scorn that
prevented it being truly beautiful.

Mr. Churchill's and Ellen's voices at that
moment called out to us, as if in wonder
where we had hid ourselves. As the housekeeper bustled out of the room to tell them,
I wondered why the other picture should be
thus turned from all beholders. I quickly
moved it an inch or two, endeavouring to
catch a glimpse of what had excited my
curiosity while my guide was absent. What
a beautiful, beaming, happy face met mine !
It showed a girl, apparently about eighteen,
leaning over a balcony as if listening to
some sounds beneath that made her very
happy, for even in the picture the lovely
face was lit up with such a sunny smile
parting her rosy lips ; and a pair of expressive black eyes were laughingly glancing

downwards. The complexion was white as ivory, with a rich damask flush giving lustre to the eye and brow—the figure slight and elegant, all in white. She held carelessly in her hands a handful of summer roses, whose leaves lay in showers at her feet. It was a lovely picture I looked and looked again, fascinated by it, just as I had been when I had lifted the veil that hung over the beautiful Mrs. Wentworth. I thought of her lying on that bed of death, and then on the happy and lovely face of this young and sweet girl. Was she happy now? Who was she, that her beauty should be thus hidden from the light against a dark damp wall, while one less beautiful, less engaging, should be hung up for all who chose to gaze freely on her?—But footsteps drew near, and voices, and Ellen and the old woman entered the room.

"What a pretty picture," was Ellen's

first exclamation, struck, as I had been at first, by the beauty of it.

" It's done for Miss Clara," replied the old woman shortly and crossly.

" And what is this picture?" said Ellen, moving towards the wall.

" Oh! *that's* only a frame," she answered gruffly; " it's covered with dust, and you had best not touch it."

Only a *frame!* with that living earnest face, bright, pure, and beautiful, as I had just seen it covered up in dust and darkness! I pondered over the falsehood silently: I did not dare confess that I knew to the contrary, and that the frame contained as beautiful and glowing a picture as human eyes had ever rested on. I looked fully into the speaker's face for a moment, to read its expression; fancy perhaps made me think that a strong look of pain contracted her withered sallow features; it was but for an instant — the next, she was hurrying

us to an open window from which a flight
of steps led us to the flower-garden. She
there left us, and her figure, stiff, grim, and
mysterious, was seen along the dark narrow passage. I watched her till she was
out of sight, and then told Ellen of my
conversation with her, of the questions I had
asked, and of the evident determination on
her part not to answer them—of the name
I had seen written in the different books
that lay upon the table, and lastly, of the
exquisite picture that I would have given
anything she could have looked at, but
which I had feared to ask permission to see
after the false answer from the cross old
housekeeper regarding it. Ellen merely
answered that she should like to have seen
it, but she evidently did not dwell much on
it, or feel that it was in any degree interesting or mysterious, whilst I could not divest
myself of what I had seen and heard. The
strange old rooms, the two pictures, the

expression of the two faces, haunted me—
fancy took such hold of me, that I imagined
some deep romance could be revealed by
that old and stern-looking matron, furnishing me thought and interest for some time
to come. As I wandered by Edward and
Ellen through the garden, I wondered why
I allowed myself to be thus imaginative and
romantic about people whom I should pro-
bably never see, or if I did, who would perhaps possess no real interest in my eyes.
Yet, I did think much of them; and even
the beautiful but neglected garden, and the
pine-wood beyond, did not call forth the
admiration it would generally have done.
My mind was just then with those two lovely
girls in that dark old-fashioned room. Fortunately, Ellen was talking to her husband,
and did not notice my abstraction. We
wandered on to the thickest part of the
wood—deep, solemn, and beautiful it was;
and only here and there through the dark

branches did we see the golden autumn sun struggling through them with its rich light. We stopped at intervals to feast our eyes in silent happiness and wonder on its exceeding beauty. Once, as we paused in the deepest and most gloomy of the paths, wondering which way to turn, and fearing to lose ourselves in this lonely wilderness as once before, two voices, rich, powerful, and thrilling, burst on my ears, and those of my companions, in words I well remember.

Mr. Daubeney and Valerie could not have been far off, so distinctly did their voices mingle with the breeze.

" I do love you, you alone, you know it, Louis ! it is but fear of the world's opinion makes me hesitate and to be for ever cast away."

" Then you lead me on thus far, to leave me alone for ever. Oh ! Valerie ! Valerie ! cruel as you are, beloved as you are, why have you thus tortured a heart already crushed and miserable? leave the world and its follies, fly with me to some region far off, where the breath of slander cannot come, where love will compensate for the pleasures of society, where I will give you all the devotion of my soul, the affection that finds its echo in your heart *alone*."

Then sobs, and tears, and a few impas. sioned words followed. I glanced at Edward Churchill, then on Ellen; faint and white she grew, standing motionless, with her lips parted, as if in terror; while Edward, to avoid a meeting that would at once be distressing and perplexing to all parties, bade us turn back softly.   We did so; and in passing a gate leading from the wood, two horses were tied by the bridle to it; I recognised them as Lord Falconhurst's.   Ellen never spoke; her eyes were averted from mine; she mounted her horse, and our ride home was very different from our pleasant ride to the forest.

On reaching home, Ellen went quietly to her room ; sad and still she looked, though she gave her thoughts no utterance ; while Edward Churchill, who had remained in the drawing-room, said—

" Inez, we have had convincing proof indeed, this afternoon, of all you have implied in speaking of your cousin, Lady Falconhurst.   Ellen's painful silence distresses me ; she should come fairly, and tell you that her judgment has failed her in this matter, and do you the justice you merit ; she will, I trust, when she thinks calmly over it. As for your cousin, she is too contemptible to speak of, except to say, that never, as a *friend* of Ellen's, shall she enter these doors ; as an acquaintance she must ; till she acts openly, so that the world will cast her off, which must be soon ; her sin must find her out."

" Do not," I asked, interrupting him, " speak of this to Ellen now ; she is convinced in her own mind, and is unhappy enough, if one may judge by looking at her face. I have written this letter to her : will you read it ?"

Edward Churchill took the letter, and after reading it attentively, said, with an expressive look of pain —

" Do you then really mean her to read this, telling her of our love and all its misery ? Will it not cause her a thousand fresh pangs ?"

" Not more than she already endures," I answered ; " watching her as I have done, I see the pain she suffers daily, hourly, from Valerie's friendly disclosure, told, of course, not as it really was, or as it now exists, but infused with the poison of her own base thoughts, her wicked inventions. Painful as the truth is, it is still the truth ; let her read it, and exercise her own judgment, not listen to that of others."

" You are right Inez, but oh ! you have

never mentioned your own hard sacrifice, all you bore for her."

" Let that rest," I answered ; "her own feelings will supply what I have omitted : many words will not alter a thing : Ellen will feel it all in time, and will write and tell me so."

" Then you have determined on going," he said.

" The day after to-morrow," was my only answer.

He did not speak, but taking up his hat, left the room.

CHAPTER VI.

The friend I was going to England with called for me early on the day but one after the scene I have described to you. I remember so well going to Ellen's door, and knocking, and her coming out in her loose white morning dress, not whiter than her cheeks, which still bore the traces of tears; of my folding her in my arms silently, and pressing into her trembling hands the letter which I begged of her to read and ponder over. Not waiting for a reply, but running down the stairs, I felt the pressure of

Edward's hand, as he took mine, on taking
leave. With a mere acquaintance I was
starting on a journey to a new home and
new ties, wishing to let the past be but a
dream, and to enter on my new existence
with a brave and hopeful heart. The weather had changed, becoming cold and
gloomy; November mists hung dark and
damp; the glory of autumn had departed;
winter's chilling breath advanced; bare leafless trees, dripping with moisture, with not
even a yellow leaf quivering on their boughs,
looked cold and dreary; no flowers blossomed
in the hedges, no sweet songster warbled in
the thickets or low copsewood. The journey
from London to a retired part of Hampshire,
was about as cold, desolate, and wintry as
any I have as yet experienced; I had taken
leave of my friend in town, and had only
two hours' journey alone when I left the
train and got into a carriage, where my
aunt's servant met me. I thought we passed

over as desolate and bare a country as I had ever seen; long wide dark fields, with here and there a village, with its church-spire rising amid tall bare poplars; wild bleak downs rose, enveloped in mist, beyond them; and I wondered if the new home my aunt had chosen was dreary as all I passed. My spirits sank as the thought deepened, but the view changed; we entered a happy peaceful-looking village; in the dim light the cheerful blaze from the cottage homes was cheering; the smoke struggling up amid the heavy air; the old church with its hallowed ground and mossy graves; the parsonage, to whose dark tiles the ivy crept and clung, mingled with withering leaf of the Virginian creeper; all looked sweet and calm, even on a damp misty November evening. Then we approached a wide com·mon, where, as usual, a flock of geese set up their screams and put out their long necks, as if in defiance of us as we drove quickly by. Some houses of a better description were scattered here and there, and at the nicest and snuggest-looking, the carriage stopped. This was to be my home: I could see it plainly, even in the twilight. It was a nice old-fashioned-looking house, with deep-set windows and very dark tiling; a lawn before it, well studded with evergreens, and here and there a winter rose smiled forth, as if in welcome; there was perhaps no real beauty, either in the village or in this old house, yet, in its quaintness and absence of all that was wild or romantic in the scenery, it seemed to bring a home-comfort I had long needed. My aunt hurried out to give me a kind and hearty welcome. Drawing my arm within hers, she led me to a nice blazing fire in the drawing-room; rich warm-looking curtains shut out the misty twilight; cases of books shone out invitingly, promising me many a happy and well-employed hour through the long winter; stands of flowers in the window gave a lightness and elegance to the room ; I looked around, and then said—

" Well, you have a comfortable home here, aunt.   I am so glad to come to you," and I kissed her.

" We can contrive to make ourselves happy, I hope," she answered, kindly, " and then, in the summer we can go to some gayer place; your old aunt does not wish to mope you to death,"

" Don't fear that," I replied, " I feel I shall be very happy here ;" and if I might judge by our evening, I most assuredly was not mistaken.

" Have you many neighbours ?" I asked, as we sat together over the fire in the evening, my aunt busily engaged with her knitting.   " Tell me about the different people before I see them."

My aunt laughed, and answered—

" I fear, my dear, the neighbours are not

likely to interest you; there is scarcely a young person in the village, and no young gentlemen; you will meet with no heroes, I am afraid, to wile away your winter."

" I think I can get over that," I replied, smiling.

" Why, are you engaged?" she asked, looking at me.

With a deep blush spreading over my face, I answered—

" Oh! no, I have no interesting love-tale to pour forth, believe me."

There came, as I said this, a painful thought of the promise I had given Charles Huntingdon not to marry; a promise wrung from me in a moment of great unhappiness; he might not, and in all probability would not, seek me, or wish this promise to be kept; yet, it had been given solemnly, and to one I did not love. I liked him better than anyone else, yet, was that sufficient to have said, I would keep my heart and hand free ? Supposing I met one I could love, and who loved me, what would my feelings be ? Musing on this, I suddenly exclaimed :

" Aunt, I am thankful there are no young men here, so don't distress yourself, pray."

" Is this the result of the dreamy fixed look you have bestowed on the fire the last ten minutes, my dear child ?"

" Not exactly," I answered, laughing ; " but to go back to our neighbours, tell me something of them."

" Well, there is the clergyman and his wife, who live at the Parsonage house, Mr. and Mrs. Mason—they are such a good old couple— by the bye, they are expecting their only son home at Christmas ; he is a chaplain in India, and is coming home on sick leave, perhaps you may restore him. Well, then, Mr. Green, the surgeon is a clever good little man, and has a nice pretty little wife, rather fussy, perhaps, and for that reason not elegant, but very pleasant and good-natured, with three sweet little children whom you will like, I am sure; then there is an old bachelor, so there's a chance for you—Mr. Grimshaw."

"Oh! what a name!" I exclaimed, laughing; "is he to be my only hero?"

"I fear so; but do not judge by a name; remember what Shakespear said."

"Pray, describe this Mr. Grimshaw."

"I shall do no such thing; he shall burst upon your sight without any description—first impressions are often lasting: he cannot fail to charm when he comes in tomorrow morning with 'The Times' paper, which he never fails to do."

"And are these few people the only acquaintances you have?" I asked.

"The only ones near; but some of the country people have called lately, which I am glad of for your sake, particularly as they seem inclined to be sociable : and now you know what you have to expect."

" And I am perfectly contented ; we shall do very well, and we shall, I hope, be very happy.   Now, really, I am too sleepy to say a word more ; my journey has tired me so ; quiet will be all I desire—good night ! dear aunt ; I thank you for affording me this happy, quiet home."

CHAPTER VII.

IT is always curious, after having arrived in the twilight at any place, to observe it in the full light of morning. When the sun shone brightly into my room, waking me, I went eagerly to my window, and looked out. Nature, no longer dark and dreary, but sunny, fresh, and beautiful, greeted me; the lawn wet with the mist of the preceding evening, each blade of grass glittered like diamonds in the sunlight: pretty, happy birds were shaking the dew off their

gay plumage, and were flying from spray to
spray, warbling and chirping, whilst, on
the wide common, my friends the geese were
assembled in a body, ready to attack my
aunt's little Scotch terrier, who barked
furiously at them. I could descry across
the common the church-spire rising mid the
leafless trees, and the old ivied chimney of
the parsonage looked picturesque ; it was
altogether such a pretty scene, that I thought
my aunt's choice of a home very much
what I should have chosen. I should, however, miss the sea—miss the soothing sound
of its waves rolling like endless music, that,
whether in storm or calm, had solaced me.
I seemed to look for it beyond the common,
and between the trees, as for some familiar
friend, and sighed. Yes, I thought all the
dreams of my youth must vanish, one by
one : realities, hard, perhaps, even revolting,
must take their place ; let the past be then
as dead to me ! What right had I thus

to raise into existence again feelings that should have been buried long ago, never to wake again? Rather should I look to the present, and improve it. I turned from the window, and as soon as I was dressed, sauntered through the garden, enjoying the freshness of the morning, till my aunt summoned me to breakfast. We remained talking over it, till a loud knock announced Mr. Grimshaw, and the only bachelor in the village entered. He was a very portly-looking old man, apparently about sixty, with bald head, small twinkling grey eyes, and tightly-compressed lips; his dress, scrupulously neat, was somewhat antiquated. I could scarcely repress a smile.

"My dear madam, how are you this morning?" addressing Mrs. Hetherington, then glancing on me, whilst my aunt in due form introduced me.

"Madam, I congratulate you," he said, "on having not only secured such a companion in your solitude, but on having given us so fair a flower to adorn our village."

His bald head seemed to glow with satisfaction as he uttered this compliment, bowing low to himself the while.   I, smiling, said—

" The village is so pretty, judging from the view out of this window, that it scarcely needs ornament."

" My dear young lady", answered Mr. Grimshaw, "your thus viewing it with favourable eyes would give it a beauty, had it not before possessed one; but it *is* a pretty village, it is all you say. Mrs. Hetherington is fond of it ; I am also fond of it ; may you too grow fond of it, and never leave it !"

Mr. Grimshaw bowed low to himself again, and settled his neckerchief.

" I hope to like it," I said ; " but the idea of never leaving it, is not altogether cheering : do you think so, aunt?"

She smiled, and looked up with such a

funny expression in her face, that I could
not help laughing.

"Ah! cheering sound!" said Mr. Grimshaw; "what is more delicious to the senses
than a clear ringing laugh? long is it, my
dear young lady, since sounds musical as
your sweet laugh have been heard here."

"Does no one laugh then in this village?"
I asked; "are you all so very solemn?"

"Not solemn, my dear young friend," answered Mr. Grimshaw, "only subdued by
sorrows and cares, that you could not have
known in your short experience of life."

"Yet," cried my aunt, "we do manage
to get up a laugh here sometimes, Mr.
Grimshaw."

"Madam, around your social hearth we
could not do otherwise; dismal faces would
be out of place: if the sorrow that gnaws
us, were ever to be laid aside, or even for a
moment forgotten, would it not be *here?*"

At these words Mr. Grimshaw laid his
hand, which was a very ponderous one, on
his heart, and sighed a weighty sigh—then
bowed low to my aunt and me, and departed.

"Why did you not prepare me for this?"
I said. "Surely Mr. Grimshaw is insane;
and, as for his bows, they are perfectly
ridiculous."

"You will have to bear these morning
visits," said my aunt. "Mr. Grimshaw
and 'The Times' are as sure visitors each
day as the light; he *has* a most absurd
manner, and is, as you say, somewhat
flighty. What he most prides himself upon,
is his politeness: if my pet cat is on the
rug, he gives place to her with a low bow.
A quarter of an hour is the extent of his
visit, so don't take fright. We shall have
all the neighbours to-day, I see, so let us
take a stroll this morning."

My aunt was right; I had walked over

the common, through the village, and
looked at the church, delighted with all I
saw, and we had only just entered the house
when a loud knock announced visitors, and
Mr. and Mrs. Green entered. I saw a short,
slight man, clever-looking too, enter the
room, with a doll of a wife by his side,
very small, with such a pretty little plump
figure, with showers of brown ringlets hanging under her little pink bonnet, laughing
brown eyes, and such rosy cheeks! All
ringlets, smiles, and flutter, she surveyed
me with a hasty glance, as she bowed and
smiled.

" How fortunate we are to have such a
day as this after the weather we have had !"
she said. "I am so glad you are come !—
it's dull enough here, as you will find out,
without my telling you. I hope you will
come often and see us, and we must try and
find some amusement for ourselves this
winter. I assure you I have been dying of

ennui, and am charmed that you have come amongst us."

She rattled on in a lively pleasant manner, and in half an hour I heard more, I would venture to say, of every family within twenty miles from her, than I should have known had I remained in the village for years by my own enquiries; pressing me to come and see her as often as I could, and cordially shaking my hand, she took her leave. She was just as my aunt had described her, pretty, good-hearted, amusing, rather too bustling to be quite elegant, but not vulgar; she left an agreeable impression on my mind. It would be pleasant to have some one to talk to during the dreary winter, and we could take long walks together; and then, as a kind of contrast to her gaiety, an old couple entered the room, nice quiet old-fashioned looking people, and I knew at once it was the clergyman and his wife. Yes, I have seldom seen people who impressed me so much with the idea of goodness, as did Mr. and Mrs. Mason—in both faces there was that look I have some-times noticed in elderly people—a look to revere as well as to love—of calm endurance of what it has been their lot to bear through life's thorny path—a cheerful placid expres-sion, beaming with benevolence for all around. When they shook me by the hand, and welcomed me amongst them, I felt indeed as if I were received into that good man's flock; and that if misfortune or temptation assailed me, I could go to him for counsel, or crave his blessing.

"You are expecting your son, I hear," said my aunt, addressing Mrs. Mason. "I am sorry, however, to hear it is on sick leave, he is coming to you after an absence of so many years."

"Yes, he has been very ill," replied Mrs. Mason, while tears filled her calm eyes. "Seymour was never strong, and I fear that an Indian life has not benefited a constitution always delicate. We hope he will be here before Christmas. I have not seen him for fourteen years, and I should be glad that his father's eyes should rest once more on his only child."

She paused; and in one glance of her eyes, I saw that rapt look of real feeling cast upon her husband which proves that there is unchanging love enduring to the end of life. I could reverence them both, and wish and pray, that if Providence had allotted me a long life, my last days might be like theirs. I longed to see more of them; and as they were very intimate with my aunt, this was likely to be the case. We had no more visitors that day. As the twilight deepened, and evening closed, we drew the warm curtains, and by the blazing fire with plenty of books, I began to feel at home, and wish for no other. There was but one thing I now longed to see completed, Ellen's happiness. I had left her sad and ill, estranged from him she loved. I trusted that time would alter all that, and that when next we met, I might find her the same light-hearted happy wife I had known her first. I longed for her answer to my letter. I little knew how long it would be ere I heard from her, or under what circumstances.

The days glided by quickly and quietly. I had returned all the visits, laughed and chatted with pretty little Mrs. Green, who had taken a pattern of half my wardrobe already. Many a pleasant afternoon I spent with my kind old friends, the Masons, who treated me more like one they had known from childhood than a complete stranger. I had become accustomed to Mr. Grimshaw and the " The Times;" indeed, had grown so polite in consequence that I feared my life would be one perpetual curtsey—so initiated was I in politeness. Several of

the country families had called. I had become quite familiar with the place, and
liked it extremely ; the country round too
(though in the dreary time of the year),
was decidedly pastoral and pretty. Mrs.
Green had kindly shown me the finest views
in the neighbourhood, and had devoted
much of her time to my amusement. I
liked joining her in these rambles : and
yet there were times when I preferred a
quiet stroll by myself through the wide
fields, or to saunter alone through deep
lanes away from the village ; always feeling, that having waded through a sea of
mud, I was, or ought to be, repaid by some
view of distant hills, some old farm house
or picturesque cottage, that, gilded with
the winter sunsets, never failed to please me.
One day I had set out alone, turning down a
road I had never before noticed, and had wandered on regarding neither time nor distance,
when from the opening in the road between

the trees, I saw a lonely house away from everything; and I wondered why any one should have chosen so desolate a situation for a home.   It stood on a slanting hill, with a paved court before it; and the entrance door was low and humble-looking.   There was a perfect wilderness of a garden, fruit-trees, vegetables and flowers, growing confusedly together.   I approached the gate, and looked over it.   I was very tired, for I must have been at the least more than two miles from home; and as I leant against the gate, sweet thrilling sounds burst upon the silence, some one singing a low sweet plain-tive German air—so sweetly, too, that though the singer often paused in her song, for it was a woman's voice and was helped by no accompaniment, it seemed to reach my heart by its plaintive earnestness. I longed to open the gate, and wander round the garden in search of this warbler; for the voice was evidently in the open air, all the windows being

shut ; but, dreading being thought intrusive,
and having rested, as the last faint echo of
the song died away, I moved quietly off. My
curiosity, however, had been strangely
awakened by this little incident ; and I determined to come again, and see, if possible,
who it was who had moved my feelings so
much by mere snatches of a song, the words
of which I did not comprehend.   I walked
as quickly as possible homeward : I knew
that my aunt would be getting anxious ; and
as I drew near to the village, Mr. Grimshaw
approached.   I knew him directly by his blue
coat and brass buttons, his great bunch of
seals, and a huge silk umbrella that he never
failed to take out though the sky were cloud-
less and serene as midsummer.

" My dear young lady," he began bowing
low, " you have been the innocent cause of
great anxiety ; so many hours having passed
since you left your aunt's roof."

" I am really very sorry," I exclaimed

" but on first going out, I had not intended wandering so far; finding a new walk I was anxious to see what it led to, and so went on and on, forgetting how the time passed."

" Is it safe that beauty such as yours should be exposed in this way, to the gaze of every passer-by; alone, unprotected ?"

Mr. Grimshaw gasped for breath, and dug his umbrella into the ground with great vehemence, whilst I laughed, and answered —

" No great cause for alarm, I think ! my charms are not so great that I am in any danger of being carried off; and to tell you the truth, if I went out with the desire of being looked at, I should come home miserably disappointed.   I certainly passed a cowboy this morning driving his cows into a meadow; but I really believe he was so intent on the dear animals, that he never turned once to look at me."

" Insensible creature !" cried Mr. Grimshaw ; "yet how could a plebeian mind care for beauty such as yours?   You will not be long left unnoticed, believe me, and I don't wonder at your aunt being anxious with such a charge."

" I don't think she feels very responsible," I answered, smiling ; " but if she really is nervous at my taking long walks by myself, I must not go so far another day without a protector."

Mr. Grimshaw talked on in a flighty kind of manner, which made me feel that if there were many as insane as himself walking about in the lanes and fields, I might feel somewhat alarmed in my rambles.   I amused my aunt greatly on my return home, repeating his conversation to her, and asking why she had sent him in quest of me. She told me that she had merely expressed a wish that I had come in, as it was getting late ; that Mr. Grimshaw had seized his hat and umbrella and gone forth in quest of me.

I went on to tell my aunt of the lonely house and of the charming song I had heard, asking if she knew who lived there; but on her telling me she had never even heard of it, it soon passed from my thoughts.

After dinner I ran across the common to spend the remainder of the evening with Mrs. Green. I found her reading a novel, looking very pretty, and smartly dressed. She jumped up eagerly to greet me.

" I have been longing for you to come, she said : " Henry was called out an hour ago, and I don't expect him home till eleven o'clock. You can stay with me till then, can you not?"

" Willingly," I said; " it must be very dull for you of an evening, when your husband is out."

" It is very," she replied. " I had just taken up an interesting book to wile away the time. Look what a sweet little mantle

I have had made from your pattern ; I am charmed with it."

She put it round her, glancing at the glass with childish delight; and then laughed, and begged me not to think her very foolish, for she so seldom saw anything new there. If she had not looked so very pretty in it, I might have held her in some slight contempt for her love of finery ; but I felt more inclined to give her a kiss than to look severe on the occasion.

" Come, let us have some tea," she said, drawing her chair to the table ; " before long I hope to have some one who will make it more worth your while to come in to us of an evening."

" And who may that be ?" I asked.

" Have you not heard," she replied, " that Mr. and Mrs. Mason are expecting their son home from India ? Every one who remembers anything of Seymour Mason tells me he was such a fine-looking young man when he left this village fourteen years ago; that he is very clever, and a kind son and good clergyman."

" And you think I shall make a good. clergyman's wife?" I said, laughing, " and your house is to be the rendezvous of this love affair, where it is to spring up and flourish? Very well; don't be disappointed, however, if nothing of the kind takes place."

" Oh! there's no fear of *that*," she answered, tossing back her long ringlets, and looking archly at me.

" You think I am the only unmarried young lady in the village, and as Mr. Mason will be the only young man, we cannot fail to be pleased with one another."

" Of course you must do your best," she answered, " to give us this interest during the winter, and he will certainly fall in love with you."

She laughed and joked for some time, then told me of her own engagement and of the difficulties they had had to contend with during the time ; then of her present happiness and her love for her children, who were, I had certainly thought, very pretty engaging little things.   Notwithstanding her frivolity and light gay manner, I could see there beat a true heart beneath it all, that would enable me to feel an affection for her, and enjoy her society.   I had fully in- tended relating my adventure of the morn- ing, and asking if she knew who inhabited the dark lonely-looking house that had so arrested my attention, and whose voice it could have been I had listened to with such delight.   Yet, in talking of other things I utterly forgot it, and the evening passed so pleasantly, there was no lack of conver- sation.   When Mr. Green came back I found it was time to return, and my aunt's servant arriving with a lantern, I bade my little friend good night, and departed.

CHAPTER VIII.

AND many evenings passed in this way. Christmas came at last; and with it came the first hard frost, clear and cold; the sun shone out over the wide common, and mantled the distant hills. The air was bracing and pleasant. I had become so intimate with the Masons, that scarcely a day passed without my seeing them; and the day before Christmas Eve Mrs. Mason met me with her countenance lit up with joy. Seymour was coming to them that very night; he had arrived at Southampton, and would be with them in less than an hour from the time they received his letter. It was quite delightful to see the happiness depicted on her face, as she gave the letter to her husband; and I, not wishing to disturb their joy, and be there at the meeting, returned home—not however before I had gone to see Mrs. Green, and had revealed the pleasant intelligence.

" Oh! I am so glad, Inez; those dear old people! I can just fancy their delight; recollect that I shall expect you and Mrs. Hetherington to-morrow to dinner—it will be Christmas Eve, and we want to make up a little party; the Masons have promised, and one or two other neighbours; of course you must go in to dinner with Mr. Grimshaw, who is as devoted as ever, poor old thing! I forgot to tell you my pink silk has come home, and looks so sweet. I shall wear it to-morrow. How I wish our room was larger, and that we could find a few men! then we could have had a dance."

" Perhaps your hero may disapprove of dancing, so it's well it is so."

" Not like dancing! Oh! my dear Inez, what an idea! Wrong to dance! he can't be that kind of man. I have heard he is charming and very handsome."

" Well, he may be all *that ;* but I cannot wait now to hear a list of his charms. So good-bye, we will not fail you to-morrow evening."

It was not without some little thought that I contemplated the remainder of a winter to be past in the society of a young man described as charming and very hand-some, with no other companion of my own age, in a retired village. Mrs. Green had so managed it, that before I knew what I was about, dinner was announced, and I was leaning on Seymour Mason's arm, and congratulating him on his arrival at home.

He smiled, and thanked me, whilst his eyes rested on his mother's happy face; only his reply was given with no warmth of manner; the same calm, cold feeling, or rather expression, rested on that chiselled face.

He answered my questions regarding India with neither pleasure nor regret. No enthusiasm was mingled with his descriptions of the fine scenes he had gazed at; nor, on the other hand, did he exclaim against the climate, or bore one with the bad effect it had had on his health. He paid me the mere civilities that a man would offer to a stranger, and rather less than many men would, under the circumstances. He was not a man who could influence me. I would sooner look on a statue than on him; for one would not expect then either life or animation, and so would not be disappointed. After a time I was chilled into perfect silence, and turning to his father, who sat on the other side of me, I entered

into conversation so far more really interesting, that, for a time, I forgot the son.
My impression was formed, and my mind at
rest.   If Seymour Mason's fascinations
were all I had to dread, I was safe, indeed.
I felt very happy that evening : I joined the
circle round the fire ; we played games, had
some good music, and with lively talk, and
a game of cards for some of the party,
Christmas Eve passed as pleasantly as I
had ever known it.   I cannot more fully
enter into each particular—things that are
not of great moment do not leave the same
interest in the mind.   I well remember
though Mrs. Green quizzing me, and saying how very handsome Mr. Mason was,
wondering at my not being more enthusiastic
in praise of him, and of my not seeing him
for some days after her party except at
church.

I must say, that each day passing with
no letter from Ellen sent a chill to my

heart; for, if she had believed in the contents of my letter, surely she would have
answered it. No, I must be resigned to
lose her good opinion, and wait till the
truth of what I had written would burst
upon her, and she could feel it. That that
time might soon come, was my earnest hope
and prayer; and I deeply mourned having
lost her friendship. One morning, as I sat
brooding over these things, not wisely, perhaps—but there are times when desponding
fears arise and cannot easily be banished—
another post having disappointed me, my
aunt, to whom I had told some of my painful story, glanced towards me with real
concern. She was not a woman with quick
or sensitive feelings; but there was much
of solid goodness in her disposition and
character. She was very matter-of-fact,
without the slightest tinge of romance, and
laughing at the very name; so that she
could not have quickly entered into all the

feelings I had lived on, or the misery I had borne in a hopeless passion, even had I told her all, which I did *not* do. For my having been unjustly treated, she had real sympathy with, and kindness towards me ; and her indignation against Valerie was most vehement.

" Come, Inez, you must not sit there any longer, my dear child, bending over that work. Why do you not go and ask Mrs Green to take a long brisk walk with you this frosty morning ? she is so cheerful, and would be glad to have you."

My aunt did not know that there are moments when even the kindest and most lively companions cannot help us, or serve to lighten the weight that is pressing us down ; but kindness had prompted the idea—and I put my bonnet on, and ere I reached Mrs. Green's door, I met her with her pretty children, turning towards the Parsonage. I told her I had come to ask her to walk with me.

" Well, that is really provoking, Inez,"
she said, " for I should have liked a walk
so much ; but Mrs. Mason begged of me to
come to luncheon and bring Harry and
Lilian, as she has a party of children to
spend the day. Well, never mind," she
continued, " come and lunch with me, to-
morrow, and we will have a charming walk
afterwards."

I promised to do so, and she entered the
gate. I was suddenly impressed with the idea
that I should much like to see once more the
lonely house, where the sweet singer had
arrested my attention ; and knowing I had
ample time, as it was early in the day, I set
off at a quick pace, rather enjoying the idea
of being alone. The roads dry and spark-
ling with ice, the sky clear and blue, it
seemed just the day for such an under-
taking. It appeared a very long distance,
much longer than it had the first day I had
gone there ; but, as I approached, it looked

far more cheerful with the sun glancing on
its windows and dark red tiling, than it had
done in the dark November afternoon. I
listened, again leaning over the gate; but
no music of any kind was to be heard. Presently a loud bark, and an enormous dog,
with a savage look and hideous yell,
bounded over the wall, and caught hold of
me. I screamed violently, and flung open
the gate : some one lifted the window-sill
and jumped out on the flagged pavement,
calling the dog off. Almost wild with terror,
I did not at first look at my deliverer; but
at the voice, the dog let go his hold, and I
started back ; what face was that ? where
had I seen those brilliant eyes ? that clear
glowing complexion, and that sweet, small,
laughing mouth, and the long black hair
falling in soft ringlets ? Unable to thank my
beautiful benefactress, I stood for a moment
rudely fixing an astonished glance on her,

till I felt quite ashamed of my silence, and said,

" Thank you a thousand times; terror had bereft me of speech, or I should not have been thus apparently ungrateful : your dog terrified me so much."

" It is not my dog," she answered in a low sweet voice, " but belongs to the people I lodge with. Will you not come in for a moment and rest? you are trembling so."

She asked this kindly, yet with some slight hesitation in her voice and manner, like one who, though not wishing to be un kind or inhospitable, would rather perhaps I had not accepted it. I noted this; but curiosity was strongly at work: this ex- quisitety beautiful young woman, living ap- parently unknown, in a lonely wretched- looking house amid ploughed fields, with no house within nearly three miles of it, who was she? Whether I did right or not, I don't know, but I followed her into the

house. We entered a small dark-looking
room commonly furnished, with faded me-
rino curtains, and old-fashioned high-backed
chairs, and one small table on which a few
handsomely-bound books were lying. There
was nothing cheerful but the fire, which
burnt and blazed up with a bright flame.
She opened a cupboard, and taking from it
a decanter poured me out a glass of wine.
After I had taken it, she stood before me,
with the colour deepening on her beautiful
face : her hands and lips were trembling ;
and she looked uneasy. I thanked her,
and looking at her, said—

" Its strange ; but I have seen you before."

" Impossible !" she answered, with such
a troubled expression, that I replied—

" You are right; I have not seen *you*
before, but you bear so wonderful a re-
semblance to a picture I saw in Germany,
that I cannot but believe that you are the
original."

As I uttered these words she moved a step or two from me, and clung to the table, as if for support. I saw that she was trembling violently.

"I am deeply grieved," I pursued, "to have mentioned what seems so painful; forgive me."

I held out my hand to her. She pressed it, then turning round, firmly and calmly she said—

"I don't know who you are: a strange chance has thrown us together, and in your face I see an expression I can trust; if you have feeling for misery, and for an agonized and broken heart, never, as you hope for mercy, reveal what you have seen to-day."

Having spoken these words, she flung back her long ringlets, and, as if overpowered with anguish, covered her face and wept. I could hardly restrain my tears; but I answered—

"If it were for no other reason than

for the service you have done me to-day, gratitude would make me silent; but here I promise you, as solemnly as though I were speaking in heaven, I never will divulge that I have seen you. That your position interests me deeply, I own, and curiosity is awakened by so romantic an incident. Often and often my thoughts will be with you, for you have interested me strangely, but I will be silent as death. I wish I had the power to serve you, or that I might be permitted to cheer you sometimes but; farewell! whatever your life has been, you are unhappy, and *that* must make me feel for you."

I rose to depart. She moved towards me and said—

" Thank you! this visit has been (though painful in many ways, still to one who is ever alone till her thoughts oppress and madden her,) like a ray of sunshine, making glad a dark prison-house with its beauty for an instant, then leaving it darker than before. God bless you! and may you never know the misery I feel."

I had my hand on the door-handle, in-tending to leave her, but so fascinated was I by this lovely creature's beauty and grief, that I turned and said—

" I do not wish to force myself on you, or to gain your confidence; but if some-times, in my lonely rambles, you would permit me to enquire for you, or see you for a moment, bring you books, or in any way serve you, believe how glad I shall be to help or cheer you."

" Oh! thank you and bless you for your kind feeling," she answered; " it is neces-sary that I should live secluded for a time; but as you have promised to rigidly keep my secret, come and see me again; not soon, however, for fear of raising suspicion, but in some little time; then I may perhaps reveal the history of a life, which, though short, has been full of incident. Think of me kindly, and do not betray me."

As she spoke I pressed her hand, and fixing one look on her glorious face, opened the door and left her.

The picture turned to the wall in that old castle in the pine-forest, and the lovely face I had just looked on, were the same.

CHAPTER IX.

I THOUGHT much of what I had just witnessed, deeply impressed in favour of this
young and beautiful woman. Whether
her griefs were brought on by the faults of
others, or by her own, I could not of course
know; but however it had been, the result
was the same. There seemed no guile in
that young fair face, no evil depicted there.
I resolved, after a time, to see her again,
and I wondered why one so young should
be obliged to live in this strange seclusion.
It was not late when I returned home, and

telling my aunt that finding Mrs. Green was going to the Masons', I had taken a long walk by myself, she did not ask where I had been. I was sitting in the drawing-room, still with my bonnet on, when Mr. Mason was announced. I said before that I had not been agreeably impressed with his appearance : I don't think I was more so *now ;* and yet I did see that he was eminently handsome.

" I have come," he said, " with a message from my mother, begging you and Mrs. Hetherington will dine with us this evening ; we shall be quite alone."

My aunt accepted the invitation, and then said—

" How glad you must be to be quiet here again !"

" I am glad to be at home," he replied ; " but, as far as rest goes, it is no rest to be unoccupied : my life in India is an active one for mind and body."

" So active that it has caused your health
to fail," answered my aunt. " I should
have thought the perfect quiet and repose
of this place would be like Paradise after
the toil and heat."

Mr. Mason smiled, and after a moment's
silence, said—

" It requires, I think, such buoyant spirits
to lead a do-nothing life in a quiet country
village; well enough for those who have a
constant flow of good spirits to carry them
on. I like to get rid of myself in working
for others, and leave no time for gloomy
thoughts to intrude."

I had remained silent during this conversation, but now, looking up from my
work, I said—

" But do you think one's mind must
remain dormant and unoccupied because we
live in a quiet place with no business to
perform? are there not duties in every-day
life that bring the mind into work? Surely

no one need be idle, and the mind can
never rest."

Mr. Mason for an instant cast a quick
scrutinizing glance into my face, and then
said—

" I can only reply to your just remark by
lamenting that we are, most of us, widely
different from what we ought to be : there
is, as you say, no necessity to be idle, or to
let the good that is in us run to waste ; but,
alas ! for the many that, in the decline of
life, can only mourn for the talent hid in
the earth !"

There was so much of earnestness in his
face, in his tone and manner, that, as the
full black eyes fell, and the fine features
seemed at length moved with feeling, I did
not wonder at all agreeing on the subject
of his beauty. He did not remain much
longer with us, but taking up his hat, said—
" Do not disappoint us," and left the room.

My aunt's eyes were fixed on my face. When the door closed on him she said—

" You begin to think him a little handsomer than you did, my dear ?"

" Yes, and yet I do not always like his expression."

She smiled, but said no more, while my thoughts were soon away with the mysterious beauty in the lonely house : doubtless my aunt thought they were with Seymour Mason.

I do not want to dwell on much that passed, or allow my thoughts to rest on what that winter brought me, though each sensation I then felt is not forgotten : distinctly do I remember that quiet evening with the Masons, and Seymour Mason sitting by me at dinner, and telling me much that interested me about India; also our singing together in the evening. Reserved, and somewhat stern, he still was in manner;

and yet, something conveyed the idea of deep feeling, if it could be got at. There had been but one person he at all resembled : like her, his feelings seemed hidden 'mid many dark clouds ; yet in the proud calm eye, the classical features, the strong true feeling under the cold severe manner, I seemed to see again my first idol Mrs. Wentworth. I came home satisfied ; for I felt secure that either Mr. Mason was of that nature that would not readily love, or, what seemed to me more probable, that he had loved once—and was his a nature to love again ? Safe I fancied myself, and feeling my own security, I did not deem it necessary to exercise any examination into his feelings or my own. We could be friends without endangering each other's peace, it would be vanity to think otherwise. As time glided by, I did not forget my new and lovely friend, and one morning I set off alone to see her. I found her lovely as ever, only more pale and thin, alone and sad, like a drooping flower that the sun never shines on. Gratefully and kindly she welcomed me, and said,

" If it would not detain you, hear from my own lips my story : it is strange and unhappy. Yet, first, give me your hand, and swear to secrecy."

I placed my hand in her small white fingers, promising solemnly my secrecy and silence.

" You have seen my picture, " she said, " in Germany, in that dear old home in the pine-forest. There I first saw the light, there I first lisped my mother's name, and gazed on her sweet face, with almost reverence mingling with my love. My father was seldom at home : he used often to remain away for weeks and months together. When he came home, he was stern and cold in manner ; it might have been wrong, but I did not love my father much. At the sound of his step I ran away, and sometimes

would hide when I heard him calling me.
I had no brother, and only one sister, three
years my senior. She was a lovely child ;
her golden hair was the admiration of all
beholders; with her deep hazel eyes, and pink
and white complexion, she was considered
an uncommon style of beauty, and thought
a great deal of. You may not believe me,
perhaps, but I was not the least pretty as
a very young child, nor was I petted and
caressed like Clara, excepting by mamma;
she would press me to her heart so fervently
and say—

" ' Never mind ; my little Beechy is not a
beauty, but mamma loves her just the same
as Clara.'

" I was not old enough to know or feel how
much more she doted on me. Any visitors
who, from time to time, came to the castle,
caressed the pretty spoilt Clara, while they·
would pass me by without remark, excepting
sometimes in my mother's presence, when a

kiss or a handful of sugar-plums would be given me; yet I felt no envy of my sister, for I loved her. There was one, however, who cared for me amid all that household, an elderly woman, who had accompanied my mother on her marriage, and had since taken the responsible charge of housekeeper. My father was a German, but had been much in England; my mother, of English family; and I have heard since, her marriage was one of convenience, not of affection: her father, being almost ruined, had forced her to marry richly. My father knew this, and after he had grown accustomed to her beauty, he ceased to care for her, and absented himself as much as possible from her society. She did not live long to care for or heed it; all I remember of her death is, that Clara and I cried very much, as we watched the awful-looking hearse that bore her remains off through the dark pine-forest, and that for long we wore gloomy black dresses trimmed with crape. Mrs. Stedman, the housekeeper, grew more silent than ever, and more rigid in her watch over us; I could see she did not like my sister, which was strange, as Clara would often caress her, and give her presents, whilst I, half frightened at her, and ridiculing her old-fashioned ways, took no pains to make her love me; yet she loved me best; and young as Clara was, she felt this, and was angry at it. My sister's nature was one I could never understand; she would never allow herself to be known, yet she was exacting of others' affection, and demanded their attention: in our games she always took the lead, and was selfish in choosing the prettiest playthings; old Mrs. Stedman often scolded her for this, but she seemed little to heed either advice or scolding. We had a governess: her strict, rigid discipline did much harm, checking in us any natural affection or feeling

we might have shown, if some gentler spirit
had guided us, softening instead of hardening
our natures."

"But did not your father show kindness
in his manner towards you?" I asked, interrupting her.

"No: he was seldom at home; when he
was, he would pet Clara, seeming proud of
her beauty, which pleased her extremely;
but when we reached the ages of fourteen
and seventeen, we were sitting out on the
lawn one day, Mrs. Stedman with us—for
our governess had gone away for the holi-
days, and we were seated on the grass
looking at the rich sunset, when I whispered
to Mrs. Stedman—

"'Does not Clara look pretty?'

"'Yes, Miss Beatrice;' but whilst she
answered my question, she looked into my
face; and, after a moment, said—

"'I shall judge between you when you
are a few years older; maybe, Miss Clara

will not be looked at when you are sixteen.'

" ' When I am sixteen! Why, my dear Mrs. Stedman, I am not pretty.'

"Clara had not heard our conversation, or I am sure it would have annoyed her. Mrs. Stedman's remark, however, caused me to look at my glass more than I was wont to do ; and it struck me that my complexion was growing quite as beautiful as Clara's : my eyes seemed suddenly filled with a new expression, and my raven hair hung in quite as glossy and long ringlets as hers. This would have passed from my mind in all probability, had not my father arrived unexpectedly from Paris ; and as we sat with him in the evening, he suddenly looked at me, and drawing me near him said—

" ' Clara, if you don't look sharp, little Beechy will be the beauty after all ; for I never saw a girl grow so handsome in so short a time.'

" Clara did not answer him directly, but with an expression half envious, half contemptuous, she said, after a while—

" ' Whatever she may be, she will doubtless gain more affection than I seem to do ; she will take good care of that.'

" ' Oh ! Clara ! Clara ! why do you speak thus?' said my father.

" She only answered with a burst of passionate weeping, while my father, angry as he well might be at such childish conduct and vanity, bade her leave the room. I soon followed her, and tried to soothe her ; but when she coldly repelled my efforts to do so, my spirit and temper, which were warm and violent, rose, and I spoke what was in my mind. I, who had always been kept in the background, was not going to be kept down for ever by her, and treated in this way because of the first praise that had ever been bestowed on me ; and I left the room with a sad and angry feeling I

had never felt before towards her. It
seemed from this time, as often happens,
that my father having expressed this
opinion of me, caused others to do so. By
visitors who came to the castle our appearance was evidently discussed ; and by looks
and whispers I knew that I was counted
handsome. I had wild, gay, and playful
manners ; while Clara was quiet, grave and
sentimental, suspicious too of every one, and
angry at my growing beautiful—never allowing it herself, and hating any one who
praised me. I was very proud, had a firm
will and hasty temper ; and I fancy our
governess thought us as unmanageable and
tiresome girls as she ever had to do with. I
disliked her so much, that I never even
tried to please her. When I was sixteen,
my father, anxious to introduce us, dis-
missed the governess : we were left, therefore, to follow our will, unfortunately for
both. I don't know if you noticed another

beautiful castle, almost joining our woods—
it belonged to a young baron of immense
fortune; he had been travelling abroad,
and just at this time returned home. We
heard of his arrival, and Clara said—

" 'Baron L—— is coming to dine here
to-morrow, Beatrice. I wonder what he is
like ?'

" 'I neither know nor care,' I answered
carelessly.

" 'Why, you are almost too young,' replied my sister, ' to care much.'

" I merely smiled. Well, the next evening
we dressed ourselves with great care, both
in white, with roses in our hair. Clara had
nearly all my mother's ornaments, and a
necklace of pearls set off her dazzling complexion, while handsome bracelets encircled
her small white wrists. Several guests were
expected. I saw my father scan us both
as we entered the drawing-room, evidently
delighted with our appearance.

" ' Clara,' he said, laughing, ' young
Baron L —— is coming; it's fortunate for
you that Beatrice is such a mere child, or
you would have a powerful rival.'

" Clara looked very dismal and very scorn-
ful, but had no time for words, as the
young man entered the room. He was small
of stature, very ugly, with light sandy hair,
weak eyes, and sallow complexion, with an
awkward gait and harsh voice; I thought I
had never beheld a more hateful creature—
yet my father gave him the warmest welcome; and Clara cast a look at him which
caused him to approach and sit beside her,
whilst I, hardly able to conceal my disgust,
sat at the extreme end of the room in
silence. If this man were poor and unknown, how both would have ridiculed him,
and even declined his acquaintance! He
had rank and many thousands, and he received a cordial welcome. He gave his
arm to Clara; but as I passed down the

staircase with another gentleman, he just
stared round with his very ugly eyes, and
fixed on me a rude gaze of evident admiration; my lip curled in scorn as I turned
from it.   He sat by Clara most of the
evening, to the evident delight of both herself and my father; and he was pressed to
come often and see us. As Clara undressed
that evening, she spoke with triumph of
her conquest.

"' He is clever as well as rich,' she said.

" And as ugly as sin and quite as disagreeable,' I answered, laughing; 'you must
own that, Clara, and, of course, however
much he would like you, you could never
love such a little wretch.'

" Clara coloured deeply, and replied—

"' Beauty is not everything : he is rather
plain; but as for his being disagreeable, it
must have consisted in his speaking to me
and neglecting you. Oh! Beatrice, why
will you always be envious of your sister,

and endeavour to gain admiration for yourself, detesting any one who admires me?'

" 'My dear Clara, are you mad?' I replied.   'I, who am a mere child in years,
what opportunity have I had to feel envy,
if I were so inclined? which is not the
case.   I admire you so much, too, that you
are surely dreaming.'

"I kissed her; but her manner was at
times so chilling, that it was almost impossible to feel the warmth of affection I should
otherwise have done for my only sister and
companion."

CHAPTER X.

" The day after this conversation, I was ram-
bling about in the forest alone, with my dog,
my only companion ; having left my father
and sister at luncheon with the horrid little
Baron. He had asked me if I was not going
to stay and walk with them ; and I coldly
replied in the negative, and left the room.

" In the thickest part of the wood, there
suddenly sprung out from among the trees
a young man in a shooting-dress, with a
gun in his hand, and followed by two large
dogs. I was so startled, that I jumped

back in haste, whilst he fixed a speaking
glance on me : that one look was not forgotten, as he passed on.   I felt he was the
only being I had ever seen whose look interested me ; and he was so handsome, and
charming-looking altogether !   When I
came home, I did not mention this little
incident to my sister : there was a feeling,
that I could not have spoken of him to any
one ; and yet I wished to see him again.

" 'Do you think, papa,' I asked one day,
' that Baron L—— likes Clara ?'

" 'I hope so,' he said ; ' and whether she
likes him or not, if he proposes, she knows
it's my wish that she marries him.'

" ' What ! marry that horrible little man,
my dear father ; why ?'

" ' Because I desire it, and it's necessary.
Ask no more.

" My only reply was —

" 'I am thankful he does not care for
me.'

" 'If he *did*, you would obey,' said my father sternly.

" I saw he was angry, and I made no answer.

" The Baron came at the appointed hour : Clara was beautifully dressed, and looked very handsome.   I noticed that before they went out, he and my father had much conversation together.   As he passed out of the hall, Baron L—— turned round, and in his singularly disagreeable voice, said—

" ' How very effective that straw hat is of yours, Miss Beatrice ! I never saw so sweet a picture !'

" 'The hat is well enough,' I answered, ' for what I want it for; but I care very little what is thought of it;' and I turned haughtily from him. Fortunately, my sister did not hear this compliment ; and the Baron, finding I would not say a word to him, began talking to Clara, whilst I walked behind with my father.   My sister was in high spirits; she delighted in attention, and if she did not obtain it, was miserable.

" I thought much of that handsome stranger who had passed me in the wood. One afternoon, while Clara and the Baron sat in the flower-garden, I wandered forth, hoping to catch one glimpse of a face that had so interested me. I walked till I was weary, and as it looked like rain, dark clouds gathering in all directions, I turned back disappointed. As I passed by a small cottage at the entrance of the wood, one that had not been inhabited for years, the rain came down in torrents. I opened the gate and ran to the cottage door, thinking there was no one within but the old woman who took care of it. I had my hand on the latch, when it opened, as if by magic, and the handsome stranger was before me ! Confused beyond measure, and blushing, I could not speak; whilst he, with much courtesy of manner, begged of me to enter.

I thanked him, and followed him into the small sitting-room, where a lady was working.

"'Mother, this young lady had taken shelter here, not knowing this house was let—I have begged of her to come in.'

"Mrs. Vernon (for that was the name of the lady who now rose to greet me) took off my wet shawl and hat, and sent them to the fire to dry. She looked at me with such evident wonder and admiration, and was so kind, that I suddenly felt quite at home. I told them I had not heard of the cottage being let, or I should not have intruded myself.

"'We have only been here a fortnight,' answered Mrs. Vernon, ' and I feel much indebted to the rain for bringing me such a visitor ; do you live near here ?'

" I told her where I lived, and my name. Mr. Vernon's eyes were fixed on me when I uplifted mine. I believe from that moment

we cared for each other; he seemed to me
the perfection of manly beauty, and his
manner calm and noble. I sat there long,
much longer than I needed or should have
done, perhaps; but as if fascinated and spell-
bound, I sat on and on, listening to his deep
melodious voice. Seeing, at last, that the
rain had ceased, I asked for my hat and
shawl, and thanking Mrs. Vernon, I shook
hands with her, and left the cottage, accompanied by her son. Before we parted, he
had begged to be allowed to call and enquire
for me, as he feared I might suffer from
having been exposed to the rain. I need
scarcely say, his request was granted."—

The beautiful Beatrice paused and leaned
her head down, as if in deep and painful
thought—and then said,

" ' I cannot tell you more to-day, Miss
Wentworth: if you are kind enough to be
thus wearied with an account of my mis-

fortunes, perhaps some day you will come again, and I will finish my story."

I promised to do so ; and after sitting with her a few minutes longer, I returned home.

CHAPTER XI.

I<small>T</small> chanced that some time elapsed ere I was able to pay another visit to Beatrice. Each day seemed to bring some fresh occupation ; and fearing to raise suspicion, I was forced to absent myself from one whose story had already excited my curiosity and imagination. I was more with my friends the Masons than ever, scarcely a day passing but something or other caused us to spend most of it together. Mrs. Green looked, smiled, and hinted that she knew what was going on ; every one knew it, even old Mr. Grimshaw had spoken of it to her; there could be no doubt at all upon the matter;

" Did I not notice," she asked, " the evident pleasure my society gave to Seymour Mason, how he relaxed from his usual sternness in my presence?"

I smiled at her imaginings; I knew I had given no encouragement; my manner had not evinced preference for him; we were good friends, and he was a pleasant companion, at times, though his spirits fluctuated more, I thought, than any one's I had ever seen. As time passed on, I took little heed of what I was feeling, and had certainly not the vanity to suppose I had created the slightest interest in his mind; on the contrary, I did not even feel that he particularly admired me. I was glad my pretty little friend, Mrs. Green, had something to divert her mind during the winter, and told her so; at which she looked significant, and said time would show. Tired of contradicting her, I let time take its course, and thought no more of what the future might bring. I often think with pleasure of the nice walks Mrs. Green and I used to take that winter; Mr. Mason sometimes joined us. I think her light merriment did him good ; for he would often lauh heartily, entering into her jokes ; a thing I fancied he could not have done, on our first acquaintance. I certainly began to notice, that whatever walk we chose, he was very sure to find us out ; but I thought Mrs. Green's pretty face, and merry conversation, had far more charm for him than my society. One day when we had left her at home, and he had escorted me to our gate, I remarked on her beauty and good-nature.

" Yes," he replied, she is very pretty and merry, with plenty of heart, but no mind."

" She is not deficient, however," I answered.

" Far from it," he replied ; " she is to a certain degree quick, but everything is on

the surface with her ; nothing lies very deep ;
nor has she any settled thought."

" No, for which she is doubtless much
happier."

" Not happier," he said ; " gayer perhaps ;
but you who feel and think so much, Miss
Wentworth, could not be satisfied with a
mind like hers."

" You speak as though you knew me very
well," I answered; " what deep thoughts have
I imparted to you, that you say this ? Our conversation has been, except on one occasion,
as trivial as that of most acquaintances : I
might have no feeling at all, for all you know
of me."

" True, you have been about as reserved
as any one could be, thrown together as we
have been ; shutting up every thought as
though I were too hard to feel with you, or
give you any sympathy."

Mr. Mason looked at me, as he spoke.

At the truth of his remark, I coloured, and replied—

" I could not confide in any one whose judgment I should fear."

" I am sorry to be so alarming," he answered, smiling.

" You are not exactly alarming," I replied, " but it seems to me you could not sympathize with the weaknesses one is conscious of ; I think you would despise them."

" Then I am indeed unfit to hold the office I do."

" Oh ! no," I answered ; " superiority of mind is essential for such an office as yours."

" Do not speak thus, Miss Wentworth, nor misunderstand me ; my mind is not superior ; alas ! it is as prone to all the weaknesses of human nature as any I have in my experience come across : if others are estranged from me, or do not seek my counsel, I can but feel it is because they think that though my calling is holy, my mind and life are perhaps inferior to their own; so do not talk of superiority; it is painful to me." We shook hands, and as he opened the gate for me, he said—

" I hope we may be real friends in future, and that you will no longer fear one who is far inferior to you."

I hoped so, though I could not feel nor believe the latter part of his conversation.

I don't think I was quite satisfied with myself that evening; my thoughts would ponder over Seymour Mason's words and manner.

———

The first fine day after this conversation, I again found myself listening to Beatrice, whose story deepened in interest, and ran thus :—

" As I knew that my father and Clara would ere long learn something of my new

acquaintances, one day, as we sat after dinner,
I mentioned my adventure in the rain, de-
scribing my friends who had so kindly shel-
tered me. Baron L——, who had remained
to dinner, looked suddenly across at me, and
said—

" ' Oh ! I know all about them ; Mrs.
Vernon is a connection of mine ; and I have
called once or twice. Malcolm is, I think,
a proud, disagreeable fellow ; what he has to
be proud of, I don't know, for he is as poor
as a rat."

" ' And are riches,' I replied, ' sufficient
to give us a right to be proud ? I think
not.'

" The little Baron looked spiteful, and answered,—

" ' Certainly not ; but when a man of no
particular note, and no money, is proud, it
is even more ridiculous than it would be if
he were rich and powerful.'

" Clara quickly interrupted him, by saying,

" 'Beatrice would never stop to consider who he might be, as long as he was attentive to her, or if he were as handsome as she describes him to be.'

" This ill-natured speech from my sister cut me to the heart ; but not pretending to take notice of it, I said I hoped always to feel grateful for kindness, and I cast a look of contempt on Baron L——, whose little twinkling eyes were resting on my face though he was talking to Clara. After the Baron had left us, Clara asked me many questions regarding Mr. Vernon ; and I could plainly perceive she was longing to see him, though she would not have allowed it for the world. I then enquired if the Baron had proposed.

" ' Really, Beatrice, what a question ! do you suppose men propose the instant they fall in love ?

" ' Well, then, Clara, is it clear to you that he is in love at all ? that would have been a more sensible question."

" 'Is it clear?' answered Clara, repeating my words with some harshness; " whom is he attentive to and devoted to, if not to me? but doubtless, you imagine his admiration is all for *you*.'

" 'For *me*! Heaven forbid!' I exclaimed with much earnestness, ' it would indeed be wasted.'

" 'We should see, Miss Beatrice,' answered Clara, colouring, ' how you would act, if it were you he liked : an enormous fortune, and able to do what you liked, would be very acceptable, if I am not mistaken.'

" 'I declare,' I exclaimed, laughing, ' I would just as soon marry some hideous dwarf as unite myself to the Baron.'

" 'Grapes are sour,' answered Clara in a low tone, but quite loud enough to be heard, as she left the room. She was evidently angry at my thus despising and ridiculing a man whom I feared she had resolved to marry. This horrid little man was continually at the house : I saw no marked preference for Clara ; and, to my disgust, I generally perceived that he endeavoured to engage me in conversation, which I always repelled with cold hauteur : his glances were so often directed to me, that I wondered Clara did not observe it. In the meantime Mr. Vernon had called. My father and sister were evidently as much struck by his superior manner and appearance, as I had been. I saw that Clara was quite smitten with him, though she would not allow it; and when my father asked him to dinner, her countenance brightened, though she *said little*, fearing, I suppose, to raise any jealous feeling in her supposed lover. With more pleasure than I dared to acknowledge to myself, I looked forward to seeing Mr. Vernon again : in a flutter of hope and pleasure, the evening he dined with us, I had dressed earlier, and entered the drawing-room, where to my disgust, the Baron was sitting alone : he looked up and said—

" ' I have just gathered these moss-roses for you ; but they are put to shame, lovely as they are, by the colour more exquisite than any rose-leaf on your face.'

" ' I have some flowers, thank you,' I said, ' so you had better reserve those for Clara ;' and I turned from him.

" ' Would she, or any one else, care to take what has been rejected ?' he answered. ' Oh ! beautiful Miss De Montford, do not always repel me thus ; you know too well how I admire you.'

" My face flushed with indignation, whilst I turned, and answered proudly—

" ' I know nothing of the kind ; and even if I believed it, it would make no difference.'

" After the words were uttered, I felt their rudeness ; but, anger and disgust at his thus speaking to one sister whilst his attentions were directed to the other, made me think him still more contemptible than I had done before.   My father and Clara soon entered ; and, lastly, Mr. Vernon.   I shall not describe that evening more than to say, the very perfection of happiness seemed my portion : those few hours, the whole of that evening, he never left my side : his admiration must have been evident to all.   As to Clara, I saw that the handsome stranger had fascinated her : trying, as she did, to attend to the Baron, I saw her eyes follow Malcolm Vernon, as those alone do who love at first sight; whilst the Baron, who treated his relation with coldness and almost contempt, looked as though he could have withered us both up in his spiteful jealousy and anger.   I shall not easily forget the expression of each face that evening.   I had fancied my father would have objected to Mr. Vernon being so much with us ; but, on the contrary, he continually invited him to the castle.   I told

Clara how I liked him, and asked her, if she did not think he cared for me.

" ' You would like me to say that he does, of course,' she replied; ' yet, Beatrice, what man is there that would not be flattered by a young lady showing her love for him, as you do? you will no doubt make him in love with you.'

" ' Oh! Clara! how can you speak thus?' I replied; ' his manner is too devoted to be mistaken, and if mine is (which perhaps it is) too demonstrative, *his* forces it to be so.'

" ' Well, don't be so angry,' answered Clara: ' if I thought he was deeply in love I should have said so, but I cannot at present see it.'

" I did not answer, for I thought she would not see it; and why? because she loved him, she could not conceal her joy at seeing him, or the blush that ever hailed his coming. She endeavoured, by quiet means, to estrange him from me, and gain his affection, though

not in a manner that would be easily discovered; yet, I think I never saw such re-
pugnance shown to any pretty woman, certainly, as Mr. Vernon showed to Clara.

" One day, as soon as Mr. Vernon and
Baron L—— had left the castle together, my
father, entering the room somewhat hurriedly,
said—

" ' I have something strange to communi-
cate; and we have all been mistaken lately.
Beatrice,' he added, turning to me, ' Baron
L—— has proposed for you, through me;
he will expect an answer this evening.'

" I felt too thunderstruck to speak; whilst
Clara answered—

" ' Surely you are mistaken! Baron L——
propose for *Beatrice !* impossible !'

" Her face wore such an angry expression,
as if she hated my being chosen; yet, I felt
that a secret vein of joy ran through her
frame at finding she was free.

" ' Clara,' said my father, ' be quiet, and

let me speak. Beatrice, you will accept him:
it is my command.'

" 'Accept him !' I answered, rising up,
' accept that little contemptible creature ! I
would sooner die the most torturing death
that any mortal ever endured, than marry
one I hate. I will not marry him.'

" ' There are no such words (or should not
be) as these in children's mouths; for
many reasons, that I cannot now enter upon,
it is necessary that one or other of you
should marry Baron L—— : he has chosen
you ; thinks *you* the most beautiful of
human beings, and will load you with money
and jewels, girl. You must marry him ;
say no more.'

" I sprang towards my father, and, with one
cry of agony, entreated him to hear me.
He pushed me from him angrily, and closing
the door, left me too agonized either to
speak or move.

" ' Come, Beatrice,' said Clara, ' don't act in that way. I suppose, as the Baron has proposed, it is in consequence of your endeavouring to attract him."

" ' I attract him ! I ! how can you, how dare you say so, Clara !' I answered, passionately; ' you know better; you know, from first to last, I have hated and despised him. If you had one spark of pity in your heart, you would plead for me to my father."

" ' It would be of so much use !' said Clara, coldly ; ' one of us, he has said, must marry theBaron ; he has chosen, in *his* eyes, the most beautiful of human beings, and *you* must be flattered, and abide by it.'

" She got up and left the room. I sat for more than half an hour, like one distracted, and at last ran to Mrs. Stedman. She had always loved me; I would fly to her for help. I found the old woman sitting as usual, with her work by the window, at one of the old turrets.

" ' Oh ! Miss Beatrice !' she exclaimed as I
entered, ' what is the matter ?'

" My face, I felt, wore such an expression of
agony that it could not have failed to attract
notice.   I threw myself on my knees before
her, and, amidst sobs and tears, explained
all that had happened.

" ' Best if you had both consulted me,' she
answered ; ' I knew who would attract most ;
I knew which that sneak of a young Baron
liked best, and what he came here for.   La !
Miss Beechy, why Miss Clara is no more to be
compared to you than to the light of heaven ;
but there's another and a better reason, me-
thinks, why you should not wed him ; you love
that young Mr. Vernon. Ah ! Miss, don't hide
your face thus, as if you could deceive me ;
look at your face, your trembling hands.'

" As my old nurse spoke, I had hidden my
glowing face from her, and groaning aloud,
felt heedless what she thought of me.

" 'Never mind,' I cried, ' whom I love ;
save me, oh ! save me ! for I cannot marry
Baron ——. I will run away sooner, or die.
They may kill me, if they like, but I will
never marry a man I hate. Oh ! why,' I
said, looking into the old woman's eyes as
I spoke—' why does Clara treat me so ? what
have I ever done to be thus estranged from
her ?'

" 'I'll tell you,' she answered; ' Miss
Clara, as a child, was lovely, whilst you were
barely pretty ; her beauty has faded rather
than increased, whilst you have grown into
the most beautiful young woman I ever laid
my eyes on. Envy wakes evil in many
hearts, and has taken fast hold of Miss
Clara's. Now you are answered.'

" '*I* more beautiful than Clara !' I exclaimed, wondering ; ' but I don't value
beauty, if I possess it ; indeed, I loathe it,
if it is my beauty that has caused Baron

L—— to propose to me. But promise, dear
nurse, to help me.'

" ' I'll help you, child, if I *can*,' she answered, brushing away a tear that would
fall down her hard cheeks; ' if I did not
love you for your own sake, I should for
your mother's. Now go.'

" As I left her, thewords, ' Poor child !'
accompanied by a deep sob, reached my ear."

CHAPTER XII.

BEATRICE had paused for an instant, as if to collect her thoughts, and then said—

" I will hurry on to the end of my story. These daily details cannot interest a stranger; they are indeed only the outpourings of an agonised heart that for months has borne sorrow in silence. You can imagine, perhaps, how I dreaded my first meeting with Mr. Vernon after all this. It was the following day, quite early in the morning, that, sauntering in the forest, with my face pale as death, and my tears falling, I suddenly encountered him. He looked all life and joy; he did not know the floods of grief that had swept my heart dry, and left me despairing. I could not speak, and would have hurried past him; but pausing suddenly, he said—

"'Miss De Montford, what has happened? Why do you not speak to me?'

"Still my trembling parched lips were powerless to speak. With a look almost of agony on my face, that I shall never forget, he seized my hand.

"'Beatrice,' he said, 'for the love of Heaven, speak.'

"I tried to articulate a few words of explanation of what I was enduring—of the proposed hateful marriage, of the anguish that almost bereft me of reason, and of my having no comforter—no friend but Mrs. Stedman. Mr. Vernon did not answer, but with such a fond rapt expression of deep tenderness, he said—

" ' There is one heart would comfort and shield you, whose life even should be paid to give you one moment's joy! Oh! that I could ever hope to gain your love! Oh! that I could dare aspire to bliss such as that would be!'

" With a deep thrill of ecstasy, pouring like a sudden stream of sunshine over the darkness that till now had surrounded me, I said—

" ' Oh, Malcolm, you do not know how dear you are to me; miserable as this marriage would be, it would be doubly so from loving you.'

" ' Then you need fear nothing. I am poor, certainly, but I will work and live for you. My own Beatrice, look up.'

" I looked fearlessly into the depths of his clear eyes, and for an instant forgetting the past, laid hold of the happy present with a thankful heart. On we walked happy and secure, till a light step followed, and turning round, Clara was beside us; she looked very grave—a strange wretched expression was stamped upon her face; she walked slowly along, talking carelessly till we reached the castle, where Malcolm, pressing my hand, left us.

" ' Well, Beatrice, do you think your conduct either wise or proper ?' she began. ' So this is the reason you so determined to refuse Baron L——, and are so miserable. I wonder you can have so little pride as to be always walking in search of a man who does not show you any preference, and who evidently is amusing himself at your expense.'

" ' Clara,' I answered, turning to her, ' lately you have spoken words that have almost made me hate you, whether said from a good or evil motive I cannot say ; but they fall on my ears discordantly ; they break my spirit and my heart. Clara, for the love we have borne one another from

our childhood up, speak openly to my op-
pressed spirit.'

" I burst into tears, Clara seemed softened,
and said—

" ' It's strange you always misunderstand
my motives in speaking to you; I, being
the eldest, must tell you when you act
wrongly.   Your manner does evince such
love for Mr. Vernon, that he sees it too
plainly; and your thus walking to meet
him, would draw down censure on you from
many.'

" ' Not if they knew all; not if they knew
what I am so happy in the knowledge of.
I care not what the world says, so I may
keep this deep joy in my heart.'

" I spoke vehemently, joyfully.   Clara
noted my words and manner; her face grew
troubled and her lips white; she bade me
tell her what gave me this deep joy, and in
tremulous tones entreated me to answer.
Struck with her agitation, divining in my

own mind the cause which I had before guessed, I answered—

" ' Clara, can you be indeed so blind as not to perceive I am beloved by Malcolm Vernon ?'

" ' Loved ?' she answered ; ' he has not told you so ?'

" ' He has indeed, Clara, from his own lips this very day. I have had proof sufficient.'

" She did not answer ; a shade passed quickly over her face ; no word of congratulation or kindness issued from her lips ; her only reply was—

" ' I can see, my father is determined on one of us marrying the Baron ; you will have to do it in the end, fight against it as you may. I have found out that papa's affairs are in a frightful state, owing to the rate he has lived at for so many years. The Baron's estate is close to our's. He has promised to do much for my father, if you will but consent to marry him. I say no more; remember, Beatrice, you are warned.'

"She left me; and though I would fain have called her back, a stone seemed to lie on my heart, and bereaved me of all power; and I wept the bitter tears we weep in our first sorrow. That night the Baron dined with us; I scarcely lifted my swollen eyelids all the evening. My determined silence must, I fancied, have disgusted him. When he left, my father called me to his study, and said—

" ' Beatrice, your conduct is disgraceful; be your feelings what they may, you are to marry Baron L——, and that soon. Ere many weeks are over, you must name the day for your marriage, so that affairs may be concluded satisfactorily to all parties. Stop—no tears, no entreaties—'tis useless now.'

"I could not answer him; no tears came,

my heart closed against all feeling. Standing mute by my father's side, I neither spoke nor moved.

" ' Girl, can't you speak ?' he exclaimed angrily.

" ' Words are useless against threats like these,' I answered at last ; ' but as sure as I am living and standing before you now, I swear that I will never marry one I hate and despise as I do Baron L——. I cannot utter before God a false vow such as that would be.'

" ' How dare you answer me thus ?' interrupted my father passionately. ' Why is it wrong for you to marry him ? You will love him in time; and you love no other.'

" At these words my tears flowed ; and, throwing myself down, I sobbed forth a few inarticulate words—

" ' What are you saying ? Whom do you love better ? whom do you know ? Speak.'

" 'I cannot,' I answered; ' my heart is too full for words. Oh! I pray you, retract what you have said, for the love of Heaven release me from this hateful engagement: it will drive me mad. For a thousand rea- sons I cannot marry the Baron : even when I thought he liked Clara, and that she would marry him, I could not bear the thought, from the dislike I had taken to him ; and now, hating him as I do, and—'

" I paused, not venturing to reveal my secret; it would have done no good, and only made my father banish Malcolm from the house for ever.

" ' Come, Beatrice,' replied my father, ' dry up your tears, and behave like a rational and dutiful daughter. In marrying the Baron, you save me from ruin, and make him very happy; he is desperately in love, and thinks you the loveliest woman he ever saw—you will have fortune, title,

K 2

jewels, and all you can desire; don't act
like a fool; come and kiss me.'

" He drew me towards him, while I whispered—

" Nothing can change my heart; I cannot love him; alter your resolve, my dearest
father, and have mercy on me.'

" ' We will talk no more of it now,'
answered my father; ' tell me to-morrow
morning that you will act as I wish, and
for your own happiness."

I left the room; but my weary eyes
never closed that desolate night: my soul
seemed torn with the agony I endured; and
my very prayers seemed to bring no aid to
my deep anguish.

I will pass over my meeting the next day
with the hateful little Baron: no scorn, no
silence, nor coldness seemed to take effect:
he was only the more determined to force
me into this dreaded marriage. At last he

charged me with loving another, and taunted me with it, saying—

" Do you think, Miss Beatrice, I am not aware whom it is you love ? I have marked him well."

At these words the colour flushed into my face, and I am sure that the angry, fiery glance I cast on him, as he uttered these words, was enough to have withered hope.

" I care not what you know," I said. " Anything you may say or think, is alike a matter of indifference to me."

He only smiled, and seized my hands, as I was quickly passing him. I snatched them away, as if his touch contaminated me: I certainly felt as if it did. As I was leaving the room, my father entered, and desired me to remain ; then there followed such a fearful scene : I shudder to think of it. All my protestations, tears, and en-treaties, were of no avail : there seemed no mercy in either of their hearts for des-

pair like mine; and when I declared that
though they might drag me to the altar,
my lips should not utter a sound, I was
taxed with my love for Malcolm Vernon,
and my father vowed that he should never
again pass his threshold, and that I should
be kept a close prisoner till I came to my
senses. I left them, feeling as if the stamp
of death, or worse than death, were on me.
I sat alone, stupified with grief; then
snatching a note which I had partly written
to Malcolm, I heard a step approach, and
fearing it was Clara, I hid my note. Some
one knocked at the door, and old Mrs.
Stedman entered. Coming in, and closing
the door, she sat down beside me, whilst I
poured forth to her the agony I was silently
enduring. Not knowing how to see Malcolm, or even send him a note, I prayed of
her to manage it for me. She promised to
walk out and try and meet him, and to wait
near the cottage till he could write me an

answer. The old woman said all this in a stiff, half surly sort of manner; but I had lately learnt enough of her real character to know she had a kind heart, and that I had been her favourite from my birth; therefore now, when there was a time to show kindness, she came forward to help me. I had to bear the wretched long evening in the Baron's society; I sat more like a statue than a living creature, for indeed my very heart was deadened and stupified by grief.

When all was quiet that night, and Clara was fast asleep, Mrs. Stedman softly opened my door, and put Malcolm's answer into my hands. The misery and bitterness of its contents I shall never forget; he could think but of one ending to our sorrow—to arrange a meeting with me the next evening, to have a carriage ready, and for me to fly with him. His mother, who had gone to stay in the neighbouring town, would be there to receive me, and be present at our marriage.

Giving me strict injunctions how matters were to be arranged, and telling me that Mrs. Stedman would manage everything for me, he trusted that our unhappiness would soon be turned into a long spell of joy. Oh! what a new life seemed opening upon me! What rapture in the thought of escape! *Escape!* Ah! I little knew the agony in store for me. Clara had absented herself as much as possible from my society; but I could see that Mr. Vernon never coming to the house, made her miserable and angry; she scarcely spoke, and had no word of comfort to bestow upon me. I could not manage to leave the castle till evening: if I could but escape my sister's observation whilst my father was with the Baron after dinner, all might be well. How anxiously the next day passed, you can perhaps imagine; the sound of an approaching footstep made me tremble; I scarcely touched my dinner; and when Clara had taken her work, I put on my bonnet, stealthily descended the back stairs, and without meeting any one, fled through the garden into the forest. At one of the openings to the high road, stood Mrs. Stedman, pointing which path I should take, and with her blessing she bade me go in safety. Soon Malcolm Vernon's arm was affording me that support I so much needed ; weak, faint, and trembling, he hurried me into the carriage : the forest grew but as a dark shadow in the distance ; flying as fast as four horses could carry us, we were not long in reaching the town.

There Mrs. Vernon welcomed me kindly : she spoke of their poverty ; but, to save me from a marriage so hateful, and with the knowledge of our mutual love, she could not but bid Malcolm bring to her one whom, before many hours were over, she hoped she might call by the cherished name of daughter.

" Oh, that this might have been !" said Beatrice, with a look of pain overspreading her beautiful features, whilst her tears fell hot and heavy. " I feel as if I had no power to tell the rest of the story; but I will hurry to the close of it."

Ere an hour was over, voices were at the door; my father burst into the room; one faint despairing cry—and I lost all consciousness. I remember nothing. What passed had to be broken to me, amidst agonies to be felt not spoken. For six weeks, I am told, I lay bereft of reason, with brain fever . When reason returned, what did I hear, though broken gently by a heart-stricken mother mourning over her child? He, the atrocious, the wicked; had murdered him I loved. Malcolm Vernon, the delight of my heart, the madly-worshipped idol of my soul, had gone from me to that world whence no traveller returns— shot through the heart in a duel by that wretch, who is now banished from his country. My father's rage knew no bounds; he refused ever to see me within his doors

again. My note to Clara came back un-
read to me.   Friendless and portionless,
I was left on the wide world alone.   Then
came a time for exertion : Mrs. Vernon,
childless, ill, and miserable, required all my
care. The few weeks I remained in Germany,
I shed many tears over *one* grave—tears that
will flow on, and on, till death releases me
from this weary, desolate world."

" Poor girl ! be comforted," I said, drawing her near me, and kissing her cold, pale
cheek ; " there may yet be happy days in
your future ; we have many of us to feel a
bitter death in life ; but, oh ! believe me
there will come peace at the last. But how
come you to be thus *alone ?*" I asked ;
" where is Malcolm Vernon's mother ? has
she left you to struggle with a crushed spirit
the remainder of your days ?"

" Alas ! alas ! she is gone to where Malcolm rests," exclaimed Beatrice. " I went
with her to London ;" there, of an attack of

inflammation, she died, leaving me her all, a bare sufficiency : I longed for country air, fresh pure air, to once more fan my cheek and cool my fevered brow : an old lady with whom Mrs. Vernon was intimate, after the funeral was over, thought of this lonely farm-house for me, where an old servant of hers resided.   I came hither alone, and have been here some time, your presence has been my only joy : in it, I have known what it is to live again ; for sorrow and death are but sorry companions at seventeen."

" It seems strange," I replied, " for your father to leave you in this position, young, unmarried, beautiful ; to what might you not be exposed ?"

" I have been fortunate up to the present time," she answered ; " for aught I know my father may have endeavoured to find me ; but oh ! Miss Wentworth, can you not ima-gine the dread of my being just tolerated at home, and treated with harshness, with no sympathy to enable me to bear the agony of living; for life now seems almost insupportable."

" I can believe it," I answered.

I remembered moments when I had almost hoped for death; and though my griefs had found no utterance, they had not been less; even at that moment I could have fallen at Beatrice's feet, and said—" I have been miserable; I have no help, no sympathy even now." But I was silent: not even to that overburthened heart could I unburden mine. Promising all the help it would be in my power to give, and taking an affectionate leave, I returned home. I pondered whether, after a time, I should not tell my aunt: she might aid this young and miserable girl, left alone and unprotected.

CHAPTER XIII.

I found my aunt and Mrs. Green sitting together on my return, discussing some point, as I fancied, with great interest.

" What is it ?" I said, peeping in at the door.

" Nothing particular, my dear Inez," said Mrs. Green : " where have you been all day ?"

" For one of my solitary walks," I answered.

" Ah ! they're not quite so solitary as we imagine," she said, archly.

I felt confused, conscious I did not take these walks for nothing, though not for the reason they imagined.

" Perhaps you think my friend Mr. Grim-shaw accompanies me on these expeditions."

" No, no," she answered : " besides, do you not know that Mr. Grimshaw has gone to London on business ? how behindhand you are in the news of the village ! I have another piece of news, too : such a fine-looking young man jumped off the coach just now as I passed ; I have been wondering ever since who he can be."

" Indeed !" I answered, absently.

" Now don't answer with so much indiffer-ence till I describe him to you."

" I am all attention," I answered, laughing.

Everything she described, regarding his face and whole bearing, was so exact a like-ness of Charles Huntingdon, that I grew crimson as I listened, and sat down turning away from her.

"I wonder who he is," I said, with perhaps some earnestness in the tone; for Mrs. Green exclaimed—

"Well, I see for once I have raised your curiosity; why, you are quite agitated."

I laughed at what she said; but, as I went to my room, I felt certain it was Charles Huntingdon, and wondered what had brought him there. I tried to talk during dinner, but the effort wearied me : I started at every sound, and changed colour at the sound of every footstep; my aunt looked at me once or twice, as if wondering what had happened, but made no remark. I was glad to escape to my own room, and ponder what the result would be, if it were indeed he, which I could hardly doubt, from the accuracy of the description. Yet, the evening passed, and he did not appear. If the next day passed and he did not come, I might feel assured that however like Charles Huntingdon, it could not be he. As time had flowed on and I had no tidings of the Churchills, I ceased to hope: it was evident that Ellen could not write. No, there was no love left in her heart for me: estranged we were, and must continue to be; I might mourn over, but could not alter it. I little knew that before that time the following evening, I should hear much that would astonish me.

With a feeling of nervousness, I set off the following morning to a remote part of the common. On I walked, deep in thought, my eyes not even raised to enjoy the clear light of the blue sky, or the sunshine that was gilding the bark of the leafless trees.

There was no quiet in my heart. I moved on restlessly, unhappy. I heard a step behind me, but never turned to look. In another instant my name was spoken, and by Charles Huntingdon. Taking my hand, he said —

" I enquired at Mrs. Hetherington's for you, and finding you had gone out, I left a card, and wandered about, hoping to meet you. I have been fortunate to find you thus quickly."

" How come you to be here at all ?" I said.

" Because," he answered, " I could no longer bear what you have been hard enough to impose on me. Inez, will not affection like mine ever move you, or make you break through your resolve ? But you do not care for me ; I see it plainly."

" You are mistaken," I answered calmly.

" Then why, when I wrote to you, after coming from Scotland, entreating to see you, or that you would allow me to consider myself engaged to you, did you answer so decidedly in the negative ?"

" Because," I answered, " I never will enter into any family that would treat me as I have been treated ; nor enter into a clandestine engagement with you, which would justify then any thing they might say against me. Yet I have not forgotten my promise to you; nor do I wish to break it."

At these words, he took my hand, and pressing it, said—

" Thank you, dear Inez! I will say no more ; for I see it distresses you ; there is much yet I would learn from your own lips, yet I will not speak of it *now*.

He paused—his lips were very pale, and his manner evinced much agitation : it would have seemed but natural that he should have spoken of the Churchills, yet no mention had as yet been made of them : why should this silence have been on his part? I could not divine. We were now close to my aunt's home, and I begged him to come in. I left my aunt to entertain Mr. Huntingdon ; I could not collect my ideas sufficiently at that moment, to enter into every-day talk. I must now act decisively : a man's feelings strong as death to those who *can* love, was not a light matter. I was endeavouring in those few moments to decide for myself a lifetime. I saw nothing, heard nothing, till Charles Huntingdon was leaving the house ; when I heard my aunt say, " You will dine with us then to-day," and his answer promising to do so. My aunt fixed an astonished look upon my face, and then said—

" Inez, your thoughts must have been very agreeable. Your lips have, however, not imparted them to us. Your friend comes to call ; you leave him with me for some time ; and when you do appear, you sit in total silence. Is it really the case, that your thoughts are so entirely taken up with Mr. Mason, that you can bestow neither time nor attention on any one else ?"

" Not exactly, aunt," I replied smiling

I had dressed for dinner rather earlier than usual. I was looking dreamily into the fire,

endeavouring to define my own feelings regarding Charles Huntingdon. I was not indifferent to him; I might, in time, love him :
he was more worthy of love than Edward
Churchill had ever been; if, when he was
left free to act as he chose, if *then* he still
cared for me, we might yet be happy. But
what was that hurried step ? The door burst
open, and on the threshold stood Charles
Huntingdon, a letter clenched in his hand !
and his face pale, his lips trembling. Only
one idea seized me. My lips had only power
to falter out one name, Edward ! and then
I waited a moment; the cold at my heart
froze up every sense, and power of speech ;
and silently I sat waiting. Charles Huntingdon moved towards me : he drew me
nearer, nearer still, with a firm yet tender
embrace : what pity shone in his eyes, looking through mine, as he said —'You must go
to him, Inez !' He *lived* then : I might see
him again ; and as, with those words, life

seemed to burst through the death that for a moment had seemed to congeal my senses, I said—

" Tell me what has happened ?"

" Edward has met with an accident; been thrown from his horse, and is much stunned, I fear," he said, looking from me, " There is but little hope for us, Inez ; this letter is from the doctor who is attending him. I am off to-night."

I only clasped my hands ; my lips moved, but I could not speak. Still Charles Huntingdon's eyes seemed to look into mine compassionately, tenderly, whilst he said—

" I did not hear from poor Ellen : the doctor says she is too ill and wretched to write : she had implored of us both to go to her. I am going in half an hour, could you follow as quickly as possible ? Perhaps your aunt could spare a servant to attend you ; I could not hear of your travelling alone."

" I will start to-night," I replied, through

a torrent of tears that would not be kept back. Leave me," I continued ; " go to him —to poor Ellen ; I will not keep you."

He wished me good bye hurriedly, and left the room—

" Inez," said my aunt, as she soothed me after I had told her the fatal news, " this Mr. Churchill was more to you than friend or guardian. Oh ! my child, why did you not tell me more of this before ? I am an old woman now; but life, with its many joys and many griefs, has not left me hard. I could have felt for you, had you sought my pity and my help : poor child !" she said, she would send her own maid with me ; and we were to start that night.—

Oh ! the weary journey, seeming as if no speed on earth could bear me quick enough ! On, on, weary, faint and ill, I come to you, Edward, but only to hear your dying word, behold your last look.

———

Gained at last! I was at the door. Not waiting to ask for Mrs. Churchill, I ran quickly to the drawing-room; Ellen was there alone; with a tremulous cry, she fainted in my arms. I rang the bell, and Charles Huntingdon entered.

" I have only been here three hours," he said. Edward still lives, but is unconscious; I made Ellen remain here; she has been up five days and nights; she looks dying also!"

" His tears fell on his sister's small white face, as he raised her from my arms to the sofa: when Ellen recovered, her first words were—

" He must see Inez; he has asked for her so often; Inez, come to him; Charlie! you do not know *all;*" she went on wildly:

" Hush! Ellen, darling," he said gently, " never mind the past: come to your husband."

I followed them softly, and we entered together Edward's room; a sign from the doctor made us pause. Ellen first moved towards her husband; her agonized face relaxed not in its misery, with a settled despair she gazed on him : he was conscious ; he knew her ; he took the little hand in his ; but the uplifted eyes gazed further on; he saw us, as we stood together ; a spasm passed over the dying face ; raising himself up, he gasped for breath, murmured my name, and died.

A week of weary watching passed by Ellen's bedside; I never left her ; no word had passed her lips since Edward's death ; she lay like one stunned and insensible ; my heart mourned for her, so young, so desolate. Perhaps it was well she could not speak to me ; my own grief was such that had I allowed it utterance, I should have broken down altogether ; soul and body would have been prostrated; I should then have been prevented nursing Ellen : now she was my chief care. The knowledge that I could help her, watch her, tend her, was the only thing left to me. Oh ! how tenderly I felt towards her, I need not say; how terrible her grief must be, I could judge by my own. Charles Huntingdon, unceasing in his watching, was all I had ever believed him to be—generous, true-hearted, and really good. He had written off for Sir Charles and Lady Huntingdon, and in a few days they would be there. The thought of meeting them was anything but pleasant; yet, how could I leave at such a time? The night before they came, I sat as usual watching Ellen ; she turned and looked at me : there must have been an agony in my face; for she shuddered and wept—the only tears I had seen her shed. She wept bitterly without speaking ; but a pity softened her gaze, and I spoke to her. I told her all that could help her *then;* all she knew—for hers was a good and gentle spirit, and religious feeling softened at last all that long quiet stony grief, and on the simple heart stole the faith of a little child, the faith that Christ loves. Prayers for him we loved rose to that ear which does not hear in vain, and the peace fell on us that God alone can give. Ellen slept peacefully that night, which she had not done for long: it was well, for my strength was fast ebbing away; I could only crawl from room to room with faltering steps. Fever had sustained me; *now* I was really ill. I moved slowly to the drawing-room, to tell Charles Huntingdon that his sister was better. I sat down faint and trembling on entering, for all was floating in a dreary mist before my eyes. I heard nothing, saw nothing, for some time.

" Inez," said Charles Huntingdon, " this nursing of dear Ellen must last no longer;

it has lasted too long already. You must have perfect rest. Oh! if I should lose you, Inez!" He bathed my forehead, supporting me; then rang the bell, and had me carried to my room, where I remained for some days till I recovered my strength sufficiently to be of use to those who needed it.

Lady Huntingdon and her husband had arrived; but she never came to ask for me or to see me. I did not want that; only a shiver seemed to pass over me as I thought of her coldness and her pride. A few mornings after their arrival, I resolved to get up. I fancied I was stronger; but, faint and ill, I sank back exhausted. The door opened softly, and Ellen entered, dressed in her widow's dress, whiter than any living thing I had ever seen; feeble and wasted, she moved towards the bed.

"Do not try and get up, dear Inez," she

said ; " your nursing me so long has, I fear,
nearly killed you." I assured her not.
" Poor Charlie is wretched about you," she
continued ; " you must live to help him.
Before you came here, before Edward was
insensible, he told me all. *I* made the sacrifice bitter to you, unjust, unkind, that I have
been ! but my punishment is sufficient. Oh !
God knows *that*, if no mortal does; for I
would gladly die. Forgive me, Inez." The
sweet penitent face bent down. I kissed
her. In a few words I told her all, only
shading as much as possible from her any
of Edward's faults, and softening all the
past

This was all that ever passed between
Ellen and me of what ever lay so near our
hearts. Often as we sat together, silently, the
same words perhaps trembled on our lips,
but found no utterance. Quietly she
drooped and languished : she did not com-
plain ; but the symptoms of consumption,

that, years ago, misery had brought to light, now that grief was doubly bitter, and utter desolation come upon her, were again but too visible. The large blue eye grew clearer, the skin more delicately fair, and the lips more red, and, alas! I knew that Ellen Churchill was dying!

I remained in my room as much as possible; indeed, I was almost too weak to bear any exertion. I had determined, the moment I was well enough, to leave Germany. Ellen had her parents and her brother with her; and after what had passed between Lady Huntingdon and myself, it would not be pleasant to remain among them. One scene that occurred shortly after I left my room, decided my departure.

Charles Huntingdon had again been speaking to me; he told me how time had not changed him, how fondly he still hoped I would become his wife; and I was obliged to tell him of Lady Huntingdon's letter, and explain how wretched it would make them if I accepted him; that it would be wiser for him to endeavour to forget me, and not see me again. It was with many tears I urged all this; for he was now very dear to me : I had seen his generous nature tried, and it had not suffered in the trial, only showing how really good he was, how sincere his love, how true his nature; therefore, in giving him up, it cost me another painful struggle, he then said—

" All this availed nothing; he had a right to love whom he chose, marry whom he chose; time nor absence could not change him; if I loved him, all that I had urged would pass by him like so many shadows; what he had lived for was to gain my love; did I think, having gained it, he should give me up ?"

As he uttered these words, his mother entered the room : casting a severe look on

both, she paused; her lips grew pale, quivering with rage she could not conceal.

" You seem to fulfil your promise well,
Miss Wentworth," she said, scornfully.

She alluded, I knew, to the letter I had
written in answer to hers, telling her of my
decided refusal of her son, and that I
should abide by the decision I then made.

" I do fulfil my promises faithfully," I replied, calmly, " or I should not be here."

" Inez, do not speak, I entreat of you,"
interrupted Charles Huntingdon; " in my
presence, at least, you shall not be insulted :"
and then quite firmly, not angrily, but with
a bold, manly earnestness, he told his mother
everything that had passed, and of the word I
had uttered only a moment before she appeared. " But one thing, mother, I must
add," he continued, earnestly ; " if you expect me to love anyone but Miss Wentworth,
your expectations will be vain. I am of an
age to judge for myself; and if Miss Went-

worth deigns to bestow any affection upon
me, I shall only be proud and happy to call
her mine. My father knows my resolve ; you
know it now."

As he pronounced these words, Ellen
entered ; in one quick glance she seemed to
know all, and throwing her arms around me,
she exclaimed—

" Oh ! Inez, try and love Charlie. I know
that he has loved you long and well : he
little knows all you have suffered, and suffer
still ; but you will be happy in time, believe
me ; and to call you sister, would be the
only happiness left for me."

Ellen wept, as she said this : Lady Huntingdon looked at her ; pity seemed, for a
time, to arrest her rage, for she said—

" Ellen, dear, whatever happens, don't
you agitate yourself : if your brother is determined to go against every wish of his
father, we must only bear it, I suppose," she

added proudly; " but you need not make yourself ill about it."

" Mamma," said Ellen, with a sudden burning of the hectic spot upon her cheek, " come into my room; I have something to tell you."

Placing her arm within Lady Huntingdon's, she hurriedly drew her away : what Ellen told her, I never knew; but, before I left for England, Sir Charles and Lady Huntingdon told their son, that, if at the end of a year he was of the same mind, and I liked him, they would no longer withhold their consent. They said this unwillingly, coldly and haughtily; wrung from them, because they saw opposition was vain, and that not only Charles Huntingdon was resolved, but that Ellen likewise wished it. The night before I left, Ellen and I stood over Edward's grave : her agony was intense; her one thought, her one hope, was, that she might soon join him : that wish, I felt, would ere long be accomplished. She was to go to Madeira in the autumn, Sir Charles and Lady Huntingdon accompanying her. It seemed to me it would be a useless voyage, when I looked on the hectic spot and wonderfully brilliant eyes; and as I pressed her to me that night, 'mid many bitter tears, I felt truly that I should never fold her in my arms again. Charles promised to write frequently; loving him sincerely, as I now did, I parted from him with a happy assurance that time would not divide our hearts, but rather draw us nearer in that bond of love, which would be only the more enduring for the trials of the past to both.

CHAPTER XIV

It was pleasant to be back again in the quiet of my aunt's home: her kindness was great, and her joy on hearing of my engagement to Mr. Huntingdon was very apparent; she had liked so much what she had seen of him and judged rightly in saying how open-hearted and good he was.

" What will Seymour Mason do ?" she said, laughing; " and what will little Mrs. Green think of her match-making being put a stop to ?"

" She will find some one else for him,"

I answered. Then suddenly a thought of
Beatrice flashed on me; ah! one sight of
her would undo any little preference he
might have felt for me. This reminded me
I must not delay visiting the unfortunate
girl; and as soon as I had run in to see the
Masons and Greens, I hurried to the solitary
house, to gain a sight of one for whom
I felt so much interest. I found, from the
woman to whom the farm belonged, that
Beatrice had been ill in my absence but
that gradually her health and strength were
returning. I found her lovely as ever, only
paler and thinner, charmed to see me after
the weary time she had spent in my absence.

"Beatrice," I said, "I do not intend to
allow you to shut yourself up in this way
any more: I am going this very day to
speak to my aunt about you, and ask her
advice what you should do: it will be
better for you in every way to mix with
people again, and if your father should find

out where you are living, it will be your
duty to go home again: time may have
softened his anger, and perhaps your sister
may be improved."

Beatrice shook her head, but asked if I
had heard, when in Germany, whether their
estate was sold.

" Yes, it has been sold some months:
your father and sister had left; but I could
not find out whither they had gone."

Beatrice sighed deeply, but gave me
her permission to tell my aunt every particular of her history. Remaining some time,
I left her, with a promise that I would see
her the next day.

It was now late in the spring: the air
was balmy, and the spring flowers that
gladdened the banks and smiling fields
made me linger in my walk home : and all
the past came back to me—how like a
dream it was ! Edward Churchill gone for
ever ! snatched away in the prime of life,

he who had caused so much misery and so
much happiness, *now* far beyond us all, and
Ellen dying! My tears fell fast, as these
thoughts gathered round me ; but one great
happiness was mine : I could think of my
future husband, not with the wild romantic
feeling I had once experienced for Edward,
but with a deeper and more real love. The
one I had loved I scarce knew why, except
that he was interesting and handsome, and
had been the first who had obtained influence over me; the other I respected as
well as loved—he would guide and direct my
future life, as only a high principled, loving,
manly heart can ; and a thankfulness infused itself into my whole being, as I lifted
my heart to God, thanking Him for this
great blessing.

CHAPTER XV.

" My dear Inez," said my aunt as I entered the house, " where do you go when you walk out? You are always such a time, that you must walk farther than you have strength for."

I laughed, and answered—

" There has been and still is a little mystery, aunt. This morning I have got permission to tell you what, for some months, has interested me."

I then related all I knew of Beatrice's history.

" Well, this is quite a romance," said my aunt, when I had concluded my story. " Are you sure it is all true ?"

" Why, in the first place," I replied, " I know by the picture that she must be Beatrice de Montford.   There could not be two people so exactly alike.   When in Germany, I heard of her father's estate being sold ; and the lady who told me also mentioned the duel that had taken place, and that the Baron De Montford and his eldest daughter had left directly afterwards ; in fact, everything I have heard agrees so well with Beatrice's story, that I do not doubt one word of what she has revealed.

" Well, then, dear Inez, bring your friend here to-morrow, and ask her to remain some time, till she knows more fully what to do : and between us we will endeavour to amuse her, and divert her thoughts from the gloomy past."

Thanking my aunt warmly for her kindness, I agreed to take the carriage the following morning and bring Beatrice back with me ——.

I heard often from Charles Huntingdon: he was still with his sister, and he wrote me word that I must soon make up my mind to lose her. She was far too ill to think of going to Madeira or any other climate; and he feared she would never have strength to leave Germany. I wrote, begging him not to leave her, much as I wished to see him: I knew the comfort he would be to her at the last, and I also knew that the bitterest moment in Sir Charles and Lady Huntingdon's lives would be when they lost Ellen. Much as they had insulted and grieved me, I could not help sorrowing for them; for Ellen I could not grieve, loving her as I did. I knew that for *her* life had lost its charm, and that the gentle, pure, loving spirit was more fit for heaven than for earth: for myself I mourned, but not for her; she would go to one in whom every thought and feeling was contained. This was a long, anxious time to me; but having to try and cheer poor Beatrice, helped me: so often one loses self in the thought of others; the practical part one has to act each day, enables us to go through a good deal. All who saw Beatrice were fascinated by her exceeding loveliness, and her sad and quiet manner won all hearts. My aunt was all kindness and liked her excessively; and all the neighbours interested themselves about her. Mrs. Green told me she wondered I could have kept secret so long what was so very romantic and interesting.

"Really, Inez," she said, "it was a shame of you, during all the long winter, to keep this delightful little mystery to yourself, and allow none of us to see this beauty; keeping her in that old, enchanted castle, like the Princess in the fairy tale.

But where shall we find a Prince to rescue her ?"

" She is too unhappy yet," I said; " we must wait for *that* a little time.   We have gained one step in getting her away from the Enchanted Castle: leave the rest to time."

" And you, Inez," she said, "leave poor Seymour Mason for Mr. Huntingdon ?"

" Yes," I replied, smiling; " you created a little romance in your own brain that had no real foundation; being only fancy, it has melted away.   Now, all this time there was a real romance going on; but *you* could see, like many other people, only what you wished."

' " Well, never mind, Inez ; you are going to be very happy and very rich,'" she said, " and I am very glad to know it. As for Seymour Mason, he will, perhaps ——but I won't make any more matches."

" You had better not," I said ; " or you will be again disappointed."

So, many weeks glided by quietly, enjoyed by us all : it was such a glorious summer, that we spent most of our time out of doors. Beatrice seemed to begin a new existence of quiet enjoyment ; if she still sorrowed, as all must who lose what is so precious to existence, she had the sympathy of kind and gentle natures to help her through it. My aunt often said, how much she hoped that Beatrice would remain with her after I was married. I wished it also ; but feared her father, if he came to England, would soon find out where she was, and take her away from us. The Masons were more with us than ever ; they knew of my engagement, and had congratulated me upon it : indeed, at this time, I had but one grief — every day I expected to hear of Ellen's death. The letter came at last ! Charles Huntingdon told me I should not have grieved had I been beside her, as he had been at the last moment, so quietly, so gently, had that tender loving being left us.

" And never, Inez, did I see such rapture on a face, as when, smiling, as if longing to pass away from earth, she died."

His letter was blotted with many tears; he had loved his sister deeply, had watched over and nursed her to the last, and now, doubtless, felt the effect of it. I longed to comfort him; and in a month from the time Ellen died, he was with us again. The peace and happiness I then enjoyed, quite made up for the many years of my life in which I had found neither rest nor happiness. I asked Charles Huntingdon if he ever heard of Valerie; she had never written to me; and in the only letter I had received from my uncle, he had not mentioned her. I never saw her name among the fashionables of the different London balls, and I wondered what had become of her. He told me that when he had seen her last, she was in Rome, gay as ever, and still very handsome; but that all the best people, that is to say, ladies who were at all particular, would have little to say to her.

" She is not separated from Lord Falconhurst ?" I asked.

" No, not yet," was Charles Huntingdon's reply—" but even his infatuation about her is lessening ; and her behaviour with that unfortunate young artist, has in a great measure opened Lord Falconhurst's eyes."

" Where is Louis Daubeney ?" I asked " Did you not know, Inez, that he died two months ago ? Among his papers were found letters from Valerie, that became well known and talked about, nearly causing a divorce but as nothing could be proved, and Lord Falconhurst, unfortunately, is weak and yielding, while Lady Falconhurst is won derfully clever and powerful, he still con-

tinues to live with her; and as long as he
does so, the world will not believe her
guilty; though my opinion of her ladyship
remains much as it did.   During all the
time of dear Ellen's illness, not one line of
inquiry from her dear Valerie!   I often
used to feel enraged beyond measure to
think of the tool poor Ellen was in Valerie's hands; vilest of the vile, treacherous
and false as I knew her to be.   I now ask
you, Inez, never to write to or speak to her
again."

"Ah! Charles," I answered, sighing,
" you need not ask *that* from me, as if it
were hard to give her up! you know I have
promised some day, when I have time, to
collect my journals, and so let you read all
that is, thank Heaven! gone for ever : you
will then learn how readily, gladly, I relinquish all acquaintance with one whom I
despise and dislike."

" Ellen told me you had suffered much,

Inez ; and for her sake," she said, " you had also sacrificed much."

" Perhaps," added Charles Huntingdon, growing very pale as he spoke, " if Edward Churchill had lived, I might have felt unhappy, and even jealous of the love you once had for each other; but now he is gone ! and let the past and the dead rest ! And yet, Inez," he added, looking into my face very earnestly, " I would sooner have the love you give *me* than all the fanciful, romantic devotion I can so well believe your nature bestowed on Edward Churchill : Years hence, if we live, I can look into your eyes, as I do now, and say—

" Little Inez loves me now with a stronger love than she once gave me ; quietly, fondly, with all confidence and trust, she gives me the warm, tender, confiding love that is more delightful to me than any other."

" I believe you will say so truly ; let us

think of these words, dearest, in years to come; and let the happy thought that they were true, make us thankful for the past that has taught us the truth in things— and let our love deepen and strengthen with our years. Look into my eyes now, and read their truth there."

" They are clear eyes, Inez; light and truth seem to dwell in them; I will never doubt them, darling."

" Wait till you have read the sketch of my life; it is roughly done; but it may be better you should read it before binding yourself for life to me."

" I will read it the night before our marriage; but could anything you might reveal change me, Inez?" he said. " If you think anything in your past life could turn away my love from you, I warn you, you will be mistaken."

In these conversations with Charles Huntingdon, I learnt the firm unbending will that would not be diverted from its purpose ; and to such a mind and heart as his, how willingly should mine submit !

It was early in the autumn : Beatrice still continued an inmate of my aunt's house ; every day I saw improvement in her health and spirits; she possessed that wonderful spring of youth that surmounts so many difficulties, overcomes so many griefs. We did not notice the change to her, nor in any way allude to her past sufferings. I was no match-maker, like my little friend Mrs. Green ; yet, a slight foreshadowing of what might be in the future was now growing visible in the great attraction I knew Beatrice was to Seymour Mason. I think the first thing I noticed, was a greater softness of manner ; his dark, handsome face was not so rigid ; the reserved manner lost something of its hardness ; and I knew that, unknown to himself, Beatrice was the cause—so I said nothing, but hoped much.

M 2

In our great security of Beatrice's peace being established, we were, alas ! mistaken. One afternoon, as we sat on the lawn together, Seymour Mason approached the house; I called to him to join us; he did so, saying—

"There are visitors coming, I think, Miss Wentworth, for a carriage has stopped at the gate; I will call in again presently."

But Beatrice held to his arm, pale and trembling : through the hedge that divided the garden from the high road, she saw who the visitors were; and endeavouring to move away, she fainted. Seymour Mason carried her hastily into the house ere the gate was opened, just in time to save her from an interview with her father and sister. I waited their coming, in the drawing-room —bowed, and remained silent.

"My daughter, Beatrice, is here, I presume," said the Baron de Montford. " I have searched for her in vain till now; perhaps you will be good enough to tell her that her father desires her presence. Mrs. Hetherington has, I hear, given her shelter for some months, for which I am obliged to her."

" You are mistaken," I answered coldly ; " it is only lately that Miss de Montford has become her guest."

I glanced round at Clara ; pretty as she was, I could not bear to look into her face ; there was the same disagreeable expression that had made me turn from her picture, and I knew the heart was cold and trea- cherous. As I looked at her, I said—

" I will tell your sister you are here," and soon after I left the room. I found Bea- trice had recovered, but was still trembling very much. My aunt was bathing her temples, and Seymour Mason stood by, quite as pale as she whom he had supported.

That was the first time my idea of his caring for Beatrice was confirmed. I told her that her father and sister wished to see her. Might they come in? She nodded her head in assent; and I left the room to summon them. I was anxious to know how they would meet, and feared her father would show some fearful outbreak of temper, and I rather dreaded the interview. They, on the contrary, with that cold, careless air that essentially worldly people can so well assume, came into the room, and kissed Beatrice as if nothing had happened. I knew that Clara was actress enough to behave in this way, though in her heart she disliked and despised Beatrice.

Her father, after a moment's silence, said —

" Well, Beatrice, you have given me a fine chase after you ! I am thankful to have found you at last, and hope you will be ready to accompany us in the morning. I have to thank you very much, madam," he continued, bowing to my aunt, "for your

great kindness to my daughter ; I only fear
she must have caused you great inconveni-
ence, by remaining so long—"

" Not at all," answered my aunt, " we
shall grieve so much at losing her, that you
must promise me, ere many months are
over, to allow her to return here : indeed,
I feel now it will be very hard to part with
her."

The Baron merely bowed ; alas ! I could
see in the expression that played about his
mouth, that no happiness was in store for
the unfortunate Beatrice ; and that when
once she left my aunt's roof, she would, in
all probability, experience the same harsh,
cold treatment that had hitherto rendered
her so miserable.   Clara turned to her
sister, and said —

" We shall remain three months in England before returning to Germany ; so you
will have plenty to amuse you, Beatrice,
and you need not look as if all the world

were dead before you. I know you love
gaiety, and you will no doubt have plenty
of it."

The sneer conveyed in these words was
not lost on any of us: Beatrice made no
reply, but her large and brilliant eyes
rested rather sternly on her sister. She
rose to quit the room, saying—

" I shall be quite ready to-morrow morning:" and after a few minutes' conversation,
the Baron and his daughter left the house.
I hastened after Beatrice; I found her
busy packing her things: on her face there
was a quiet, still sorrow that was very painful to look upon.

" Beatrice," I said, " you must not leave
us long; my aunt, you know, will be delighted to have you; and next spring I
shall hope you will be our guest for some
time: you must not be unhappy any
longer."

" My fear is," she replied, " that I shall

never see any of you again; the future
seems so dreary, and returning to a country
where all the past has been so miserable, is
very torturing to me : however, it is my
duty to go—God will not desert me."

That evening passed very gloomily to us
all. My aunt told Beatrice again and
again that she should always find a home
with her ; and though it was of course her
duty to return to her father, it was no
reason she should remain, if she were again
treated as she had been formerly : therefore, with a lighter heart and better hope
for the future, she quitted us the following
day. It did not escape me, how unhappy
Beatrice's departure rendered Seymour
Mason, though he said less than any of us.

CHAPTER XVI.

WINTER and spring have passed away; early summer has come at last; over the wide meadows comes the breath of morning, fragrant with the scent of newly-mown hay; the foliage is bright and fresh, and the roses are in full bloom. To-morrow will be our wedding-day; and I must not remain here, dreaming my time away, for we are expecting guests. We have been here a week; and certainly Sir Charles Hunting-. don is kind in lending my aunt this pretty cottage for the wedding, so near Charles's

home, too, makes it pleasant. More than a
year has passed since Edward Churchill left
us. Oh! as I sit here musing, how I long
to know whether his spirit rests at last!
Looking along the cliff, I see the little
home nestled amid the trees, where I loved
and suffered so much. (Miss Churchill is
still there.) All *that* has passed away; but
as I gaze up into the heavens, that mysterious thought pervades my being—do the
dead rest? does the spirit ever sleep? and
where is that unknown land, where, for
aught we know, their eyes may rest on us,
though ours can see them no more? This
very evening I give Charles this manuscript
to read; ah! how faulty will he think his
little Inez in reading it! I think my hands
will tremble as I place it in his, fearful for
the future that might change his love, if
what is here revealed displease him. I will
give it in the dusk, when the stars are be-
ginning to shine, and all seems resting in

this troubled world. This will be a busy day ; already I hear voices on the stairs ; the Masons and Mrs. Green have come, and soon I hope to welcome Beatrice : this will be a trying day to my poor uncle ! I long to ask him if he knows anything of Valerie —his never mentioning her in his note, looks strange. It has been so pleasant this afternoon, sitting with my kind old friends, and having Beatrice again amongst us ! Hers has not been a pleasant existence with her father ; but Clara has, fortunately for us all, married a French marquis, so Beatrice may be able to get on better with her father than hitherto ; she seems very thankful to him for permitting her to come to our marriage, and what a lovely brides- maid she will make ! Mrs. Green has been feasting her eyes all this afternoon on my wedding dress and trousseau, looking as bright and pretty as ever : I only wish Mr. Green could have spared time to have been

also present at our wedding.   I hear a carriage driving up the road; it must be
Colonel Wentworth, and I will run down
quietly and receive him in the study; for
he may have much to say that he would
not speak of before people   .

My uncle looked tired and worn; his
handsome face is marked by deep lines,
not so much of age as of sorrow and care;
he received me affectionately, and yet, with
such quiet grief, that my heart bled for
him.   Thinking it necessary to say something of Valerie, I merely said, I wished
for his sake she could have been present;
but as she was still living abroad, I knew
that an invitation would be merely a compliment, and so I had not sent one.

" Inez," he answered, " do not name
her to me; the bitterest woe a parent can
have is an ungrateful child.   I idolized
Valerie; I gave her my care, my time, my
every thought : I only cared for riches that

she might spend them; for gaiety, that it might amuse her. I believed and trusted her, long after every one else had deserted her, and how has it ended!"

My uncle paused, covering his face, hiding from me the pain he endured in telling me this, whilst I answered—

" But she may improve; we should never despond, but pray for those who wrong us, and themselves too, by the life they lead who knows, but if we hope and pray, that God will soften Valerie's heart, and change her life. We must not quite give her up; even in the eyes of the world it would not be policy to do so."

" Do you not know, Inez, that Lord Falconhurst is separated from her?"

" No," I answered, " I had no t heard it.

" Well, he has; and no one can blame him; for though he has not quite proof enough of her guilt for a divorce, he knows sufficient of her charact·r now to wish for a separation. Not only her disgraceful conduct with Louis Daubeney is well known, but her life at the present time is such that no respectable people can uphold her. Lord Falconhurst is a generous, manly fellow : after Valerie's unprincipled conduct with the artist, he said he would freely forgive her, if her life for the future was what it should be ; if she would give up all flirtation, and would become truthful in heart and gentle in manner : but Valerie only laughed at him, insulted him to his face, and said, " a separation would not make her at all unhappy ; she had plenty of friends in the gay world, ready and willing to uphold her ; her own fortune having been settled on her, she did not need any of his wealth :" and she left him, haughty and self-willed as ever. She is now residing in Paris, the gayest of the gay, among a set that I once hoped and believed my child would have never come in contact with.

Finding my letters of no avail, I have ceased
to write to her : perhaps, some day, when
no one will speak to her, she may gladly
come to her father's house ; she is my own
flesh and blood, therefore my home will be
hers whilst I live."

I pressed my uncle's hand ; for I could
not comfort him ; I saw he mourned as
those who have no hope. It seemed a desolate thought that, as age crept on, his
hearth and home would be lone and sad ;
no young gay voices resounding through the
old halls, no child or grandchild to shed
sunshine on his latter days ! weary, and
long in loneliness and grief, must his old
age pass on, till death close his eyes in the
sleep that wakes to eternity.

———

I am married ; bright morning has come
and gone : bride, bridegroom, guests, and

bridesmaids have done their parts in the ceremony; and if I mistake not, two of the guests will soon be chief actors in a similar scene.

———

Sitting by my husband's side, I ask—

" Charles, are you sure you read attentively what I placed in your hands yesterday? you have made no comment or remark; you have only married me."

" Thus proving to you, my little wife, that I am satisfied. Together, let us pass through this troublesome world. strong in each other's love, and thankful to Him who has blessed that love to both."

THE END.

Published by T. C. Newby, 30, *Welbeck Street, Cavendish Sq.*